The
BETRAYED
FIANCÉE

The AMISH *Millionaire*
PART 3 — OF 6

WANDA *&*
BRUNSTETTER
& JEAN BRUNSTETTER

The

BETRAYED
FIANCÉE

SHILOH RUN PRESS
An Imprint of Barbour Publishing, Inc.

30938 8260
R

Cover design: Müllerhaus Publishing Arts Inc., www.mullerhaus.net
Cover photography: Richard Brunstetter III; RBIII Studios

Published by Shiloh Run Press, an imprint of Barbour Publishing, Inc.,
P.O. Box 719, Uhrichsville, Ohio 44683, www.shilohrunpress.com

*Our mission is to publish and distribute inspirational products offering
exceptional value and biblical encouragement to the masses.*

Member of the
Evangelical Christian
Publishers Association

Printed in the United States of America.

CHAPTER 1

Akron, Ohio

Thunder and lightning streaked across the sky as Joel waited for Kristi to let him in. If not for the jacket he'd thought to put on before leaving home, he'd be drenched from this deluge of rain.

"Quick, come inside before you get any wetter," Kristi said as she opened the door. "Let me get a towel so you can dry off."

Joel handed her his jacket and waited until she returned. "Thanks." He dried his face, blotted his hair, and ran the towel over the front of his legs. Before they walked into the living room, he kicked off his wet shoes.

"You look tired. Did you have a busy day?"

He reached up to rub the back of his neck and groaned. "Busy, but unproductive."

She tipped her auburn head to one side, looking at him with curious blue eyes. "What do you mean?"

"Let me get off my feet, and I'll tell you about it."

"No problem. Supper is ready, but it can wait a few minutes." Kristi gestured to the couch. "Let's sit so we can talk."

Joel took a couple of shuffled steps toward the couch but turned back to her when his stomach growled. "Are you sure? I don't want to spoil the meal you cooked."

She shook her head. "It's fine, Joel. The Crock-Pot's on low so the food will stay warm."

Joel grabbed the arm of the sofa and took a seat, reaching over his shoulders to place a throw pillow behind his head. When Kristi sat beside him, he took her hand, wrapping his fingers around hers. After a day like he'd had, it felt good to sit beside the woman he loved and relax for a bit.

"So tell me about your busy day," she prompted. "Why was it unproductive?"

Joel sighed as he closed his eyes and leaned against the pillow. Should he tell her what all had gone on today? What would be the point? It was his mess, not hers. "Never mind, Kristi. On second thought, I'd rather not to talk about my day right now. I'd like to enjoy the evening with you." He turned his head and gave her a gentle kiss. "Truthfully, I am kind of hungry, so why don't we eat?"

Hands dropping to her sides, she rose from the couch. "The table's been set, and it'll only take me a couple of minutes to bring out the food."

"Is there anything I can do to help?" Joel offered.

"No, stay where you are and relax. I'll call you when the food's on the table."

Joel didn't argue. He was beat and felt hollow. He'd bid on four different jobs today, with no guarantee he'd get any of them. He'd also finished up a small job, but the people asked him to bill them, saying they didn't have the money right now. He clenched his fists. *They should have told me they couldn't pay right away before I started the job. I was countin' on the money.* At least he'd finished working before the storms broke loose. One nasty front after another had gone through the state, but on the way here, the station on his car radio announced the storms would be ending soon.

Joel rubbed his finger across the top of the end table next to the couch, noticing there wasn't a speck of dust. Kristi was an immaculate housekeeper. Her condo was always clean and orderly. His fiancée was warm and caring, and when she looked deeply into his eyes, he could feel her love. To Joel, Kristi was perfect in every way and would be the ideal wife—if the day ever came they could be married. If things didn't shape up with his finances soon, they may never be able to set a wedding date. No matter how many times Joel tried to think positive, his financial situation always jumped in the way. The only thing right in his life was Kristi, but their relationship could end if she learned every truth about him.

Joel's eyes grew heavy while he waited for Kristi. He released a warm yawn and stretched out on the sofa. If she didn't call him to eat soon, he might fall asleep.

"Everything's ready now."

Joel's eyes snapped open. "Okay." He stood slowly and followed Kristi into the dining room, taking a seat beside her.

She clasped his hand tenderly and smiled. "Would you like to pray this time, Joel?"

"Uh. . ." His throat constricted as Kristi watched him intently. "Why don't you do it? I like hearing you pray."

Kristi's lips pressed tightly together. "You never pray, Joel. Is there a reason?"

Joel felt trapped—like a mouse getting caught in a trap with nowhere to run—as he struggled to get his breath. He moistened his lips. "I pray silently. It's the way I've always prayed." It was halfway true. Joel's family prayed silently, as most Amish did, but Joel hadn't lifted many prayers—silent or otherwise—since he left home.

I don't have time to waste on prayer, he thought. *Even if I did, what good has it done in the past?* Joel had talked to God plenty of times while he was growing up, but he'd mostly prayed because everyone else in his family expected him to. He remembered when his mother had gathered him and his siblings together and taught them the purpose of prayer. She used to say God answered and rewarded prayers offered in persistent faith— meaning prayer should be continued until something happened. But none of his prayers were answered, even when he was persistent.

He wasn't about to share his thoughts with Kristi, however. Kristi's religion was important to her, like it had been to Joel's mother. Joel was sure Kristi would break things off with him if she knew where he stood spiritually. Oh, he would keep going to church with her on Sundays, but Joel didn't think he needed religion to get what he wanted in life.

"Okay, if you'd rather, I'll pray." Kristi bowed her head, and Joel did the same. He felt a twinge of guilt when she prayed for him, asking God to bless his life and thanking Him for this time they had together. *The love of my life prays for me; yet my life is only getting worse, it seems.*

When Kristi finished praying, she released

Joel's hand and passed him the platter of meat. "It should be nice and tender, since it's been slow-cooking all day while I was at work. Even if the storm had knocked out the power, dinner would still have been good and hot."

"It's raining a little yet, but at least the worst of the storm has passed." Joel looked toward the window before pointing to the center of the table. "Are the candles because you thought the lights might go out?"

"Partly. I also like eating by candlelight. Don't you?"

"It is sort of relaxing," he agreed.

"To me, it's romantic." Kristi offered him a playful smile.

Joel noticed how Kristi's blue eyes sparkled as he cut a piece of beef and took a bite. "It's good, Kristi. My compliments to the chef."

She handed him the bowl of carrots and potatoes. "Why, thank you, sir. Now try some of these."

Joel spooned some onto his plate and passed it back to her. Kristi was a good cook, and he was glad she'd invited him for supper this evening.

"What did you think of the information·I gave you on Sunday?" Kristi asked.

"What information?" Joel reached for his glass of water and took a drink.

"The brochures I got at the marriage seminar on Saturday." Kristi forked a piece of carrot. "Remember, you were going to look them over so we could talk about it tonight."

"Oh, yeah." Joel stared at his plate. "Sorry, Kristi, but I was too tired Sunday evening, and Monday I worked late and fell into bed a few minutes after I got home."

"So you haven't looked at any of the information?"

"No."

Her shoulders drooped. "I was hoping we could talk about it now."

"We can. You can tell me whatever you learned."

Kristi blotted her lips with a napkin. "Oh, we learned a lot. Let's see. . . . Where do I begin?"

"Guess you can start at the beginning. What was one thing you learned?"

"The speaker pointed out how necessary it is for married couples to have good communication."

"Makes sense to me."

"He also stressed the importance of honesty and trust."

Joel nearly choked on the piece of potato he'd put in his mouth. He and Kristi weren't married yet, but he'd already been dishonest with her. First in not telling her about his family. Second, he'd bought a classic car and kept it hidden in his shop. And last, he'd taken money from their joint savings account without her knowledge. Joel felt like a heel, but if Kristi knew what he'd done, she'd probably break up with him. The best thing he could do was get the money back in the savings account as soon as possible.

His jaw tightened. *I could have taken care of the problem if my dad would've loaned me some money.*

"Joel, have you been listening to me?" Kristi nudged his arm.

"Uh, sorry. Guess I was zoning out. What was it you were saying?"

"I was telling you how the speaker explained about the importance of a couple spending quality time together."

"You mean like we're doing now?"

"Yes, but I'm not sure you're with me. You seem preoccupied tonight."

Joel blew out his breath. "I have a lot on my mind. But you're right. I should be paying attention to what you're saying. Go ahead, Kristi."

As they continued to eat, she shared with Joel more of what she'd learned at the marriage seminar. When they were done, Joel helped Kristi clear the table and do the dishes, thinking he might redeem himself.

When the dishes were done, they returned to the living room to visit and watch TV until they felt ready for dessert.

They had no more than gotten comfortable on the couch when Joel's cell phone rang. Pulling it from his pocket and looking at the caller ID, he realized it was his sister Elsie. Joel had no desire to be interrupted, and he certainly didn't want Kristi knowing who the call was from, so he let it go to voice mail.

Later, when Kristi went to the kitchen to get their dessert, Joel hurriedly accessed his voice mail, to listen to his sister's message.

"Joel, it's Elsie." Her voice sounded shaky. "There's no easy way to tell you this, but. . ." Elsie's silence made the hairs on the back of Joel's neck rise. "Dad is dead."

He's dead. No, that can't be. I must've misheard her message.

Joel shuddered when he heard a sharp intake of breath before his sister continued. "Dad was up in his tree house, and he. . ." Elsie's voice broke. "He got hit by lightning. Please call as soon as you can. We need to talk about the funeral."

Joel's arms went limp as he lowered the phone to the couch. Seconds seemed like hours while he slowly shook his head, trying to grasp his sister's words and let them sink in. He felt as if he'd been the one hit by a bolt of lightning. It didn't seem possible. Dad couldn't be dead. Joel's body felt numb. *What was Dad doing in a tree house?*

Kristi returned to the living room with two pieces of apple pie but stopped suddenly when she saw Joel sitting still, a vacant look in his eyes. Her stomach quivered as she rushed over to him. "What's wrong, Joel?" She set the serving tray on the coffee table and took a seat beside him. "You look upset."

He gave no response.

"Joel, you're scaring me." She touched his arm. "What is it?"

"Huh?" Joel blinked, as though coming out of a daze.

"Are you upset about something?"

Joel squeezed his eyes shut then opened them again. "My dad's gone," he mumbled. "He—he passed away after being struck by lightning." He picked up his cell phone. "My sister left a message."

Kristi covered her mouth to stifle a gasp. "Oh, Joel, I am so sorry."

"I'll have to go to the funeral."

"Of course. I'll go with you."

Joel shook his head. "No, you don't need to go. You didn't even know my dad, and—"

"It's because you never wanted me to. I've asked many times to meet your family, but you've always said no."

Joel shrugged his shoulders. "I didn't see any reason for you to meet them. Like I told you before, they're different. I don't think you'd be comfortable around them."

Before Kristi could respond, Joel stood. "I have to go now. I'm tired, and I need to call my sister back and let her know I'll be there for Dad's funeral. In fact, I should go the day before, for the viewing."

"Okay, but I'm going with you to the funeral, Joel."

He shook his head more vigorously. "I told you, it's not necessary."

She stood, looking up at him with determination. "It is to me. If I'm going to become your wife someday, then it's time for me to meet your family and pay my respects."

He continued to shake his head.

"I don't understand why you're pushing me away and why you would object to me going to your father's funeral. Are you ashamed of me?" She crossed her arms.

"No, of course not."

"Maybe we shouldn't get married, if you don't want your family to meet me."

Joel pulled her into his arms. "I'm sorry, Kristi. If it means that much, you can go." He stroked the top of her head.

Joel's hugs were always so affectionate. Although they'd had their share of disagreements, every time he held her in his arms, Kristi knew he cared.

Millersburg, Ohio

When Elsie left the phone shack after making several calls, her legs trembled so badly she could hardly walk. While she hadn't spoken with anyone in their district directly, she'd left messages about Dad's untimely death. That had been difficult enough. She could hardly believe he was gone.

After walking through puddles she barely noticed, then trudging slowly up the stairs to her porch, Elsie entered the house and closed the door. Leaning against it for support, she heard the rain continuing to fall, even though the worst of the storm had finally passed.

"Did you call everyone on the list?" her husband asked when she joined him in the living room.

Elsie nodded slowly as she took a seat

beside him on the couch.

"How about Joel? Did you get a hold of him?"

"He didn't answer his phone, but I left a message." Elsie leaned her head on John's shoulder for support. She felt drained and woeful as she slouched on the sofa. "Oh John, I can't believe Dad is gone. I can only imagine how horrible it was when Arlene and Larry stopped by his place earlier this evening and found Dad's body." She choked on the sob rising in her throat.

John pulled Elsie into his arms, gently rubbing her back. "I can't understand what he was doing up in his tree house during such a storm."

"Maybe it wasn't storming when he climbed up. It rained awhile before the *dunner* and *wedderleech* came upon us."

"Could be. I don't think your *daed* would have taken any chances if he'd known he was in danger of being struck by lightning."

Elsie sniffed. "I need to go upstairs and tell the *kinner*, but it won't be easy. All of our children loved their *grossdaadi* so much."

"I know," John agreed. "It won't be easy, but we can take comfort with the assurance of knowing he's at peace and in heaven with your *mamm*." He stood and held out his hand.

"If you'd like, I'll go up with you."

Elsie nodded. Some folks who didn't know the Lord personally did not have such hope. She couldn't imagine how horrible it must be. If not for her faith and trust in God, she wouldn't be able to deal with any of life's tragedies.

CHAPTER 2

"Listen, Kristi. There's something I need to tell you." Joel hesitated as they headed south on I-77 early Friday morning.

"What is it?" Kristi wondered why Joel was being so evasive. He hadn't told her exactly what town his dad lived in, only that he lived south of Akron.

"Umm... It's about my family. Remember when I told you they were different?"

"I remember, but you never explained in what way they are different from me."

"The thing is...." Joel glanced over at her and then quickly looked back to the road. "They're Amish."

Kristi's eyes opened wide. "Your family is Amish?"

"Yes."

"So what you're saying is all this time I've been dating an Amish man without being aware of it?" She blinked rapidly as a rush of adrenaline tingled through her body.

"I used to be Amish, but not anymore." Joel gripped the steering wheel so tightly his knuckles turned white. "I left the Amish faith seven years ago."

"So you speak Pennsylvania Dutch and everything?"

"*Jah*. It means yes."

Kristi's thoughts were all over the place, wondering why Joel had kept this from her and what made him leave the Amish faith. She glanced at him, then looked at the dashboard, unable to form a response.

"Kristi, did you hear me?" Joel's voice sounded strained.

"Yes, I heard." Kristi swallowed hard, struggling not to cry. Apparently, this man she'd come to care for so deeply wasn't the person she knew. No wonder Joel hadn't wanted her to meet his family and kept saying they were different. Did he think she was so shallow she couldn't have accepted his heritage?

"Don't you have anything to say?" Joel placed his hand over Kristi's and tenderly held her fingers.

Feeling a painful tightness in her throat, Kristi pulled away from his grasp, bringing her arms close to her chest. "Joel, would you please pull over?"

Up ahead, he found a safe place to pull off the road and then turned off the ignition.

She rubbed her temples, trying to comprehend his startling confession. "Look at me, Joel." Kristi waited until she had his full attention. "I can't believe you would lie about something so important."

"I—I didn't lie. I just didn't volunteer the information."

"Why was it necessary to keep this from me?" Her forehead wrinkled.

He shrugged, looking toward the highway. "I—I don't know. Guess I assumed you might be uncomfortable around my family and wouldn't understand why I gave up the Amish way of life."

Kristi reached out and touched his chin, turning him to face her. "Why did you?"

Joel raked shaky fingers through the side of his hair and groaned. "I wanted something more than the Plain life could offer."

"Like what?"

He tapped the steering wheel a couple of times. "A car, for one thing. I had one when I went through my *rumschpringe*, and it was hard to give it up."

"Rumschpringe? What's that?"

"It means 'running around.' It's a time when young people who have grown up in an Amish home have the chance to explore the world outside their faith." Joel cleared his throat. "Then they have the right to choose between joining the Amish church or going English."

"So you went English."

He nodded. "But not till after I'd joined

21

the Amish church, which, of course, made it worse when I left."

Kristi massaged the bridge of her nose and sighed. After her shopping trip to Holmes County with her mother, she'd done a little reading about the Amish culture and remembered one article stating how hard it was on a family when one of them left the faith. No wonder Joel prayed silently and not out loud. This also explained why he was able to find Bible passages easily whenever they went to church and followed the pastor's message. *I should have questioned him more about it.*

"Did you ever plan to tell me your family is Amish, or did you only blurt it out now because we're on our way to your father's funeral?" Kristi tried not to let her irritation show, but this was unnerving.

Joel remained silent for several seconds. "I—I would have told you eventually, but I was worried about how you'd respond."

"I would have dealt with it better if you'd told me right away." Kristi's muscles tightened.

"I'm sorry, Kristi. I didn't think you'd understand, and I was wrong to assume how you'd react."

"All I know is you weren't honest with me, and that bothers me a lot."

His ears reddened. "Look, can we talk about this later? It's gonna take all my strength to get through the funeral today."

Kristi felt bad about being pushy, but she wanted to know everything Joel kept hidden from her. *I have to be considerate of his feelings right now. If one of my parents passed away unexpectedly, I'd want him to do the same.*

She sighed, slipping down a bit in her seat. *But it's difficult to be supportive when he's kept his family hidden from me for so long—especially since I've told him everything about my family, and even shared some things from my childhood. I wish I'd have met Joel's father and known what kind of person he was.*

Kristi pushed herself back up with her elbows to get repositioned in her seat. In sympathy, she placed her hand on Joel's arm. "Today will be difficult, but God will help you endure the pain."

Joel made no comment as he started the car and pulled back onto the road.

"Is your mother still alive?" Kristi spoke quietly, hoping Joel wouldn't be upset with all her questions.

He shook his head. "She had a heart attack and died two years ago."

"I'm sorry, Joel." Kristi couldn't imagine losing both of her parents, especially in such a short span of time. "You had said it was your sister who called with the news of your father's death. Do you have other siblings?"

"I have three sisters—Elsie, Arlene, and Doris. They're all older than me." Joel changed lanes to pass a slow-moving vehicle.

"Where do they live?"

"Arlene and her family live in Farmerstown. Doris lives in Berlin with her husband, Brian. Elsie, the oldest, lives in Millersburg. Oh, and my dad lived in Charm." Joel rubbed the back of his neck. "That's where I went for the viewing yesterday. The funeral will be held there today as well."

"I see." Kristi had wanted to attend the viewing with Joel, but didn't want to ask for two days off in a row. They were shorthanded at the nursing home right now, and one of the other nurses who normally worked Saturdays had traded with Kristi so she could attend the funeral.

"In case you don't know, Amish church services, weddings, and funerals are held in church members' homes or in one of their outside buildings. Sometimes they rent a large tent if there isn't room to accommodate everyone indoors. So no church or funeral home is used at any Amish funeral," Joel explained.

Kristi gripped her armrest as he increased

the speed. Now he'd begun passing everyone on the highway, probably to make sure they got to the funeral on time. Trying to keep her mind off how fast Joel was driving, Kristi thought more about the Amish. She had read something concerning their funerals, as well, but experiencing an Amish funeral service firsthand would enlighten her further. But she couldn't help wondering if Joel's sisters knew about her and how they would accept an outsider.

            ⚜

Charm, Ohio

The only thing in their favor today was the weather. Although the sky was gray, at least it wasn't raining. As they drew closer to his father's house, Joel's palms became sweaty, and his heart pounded. In addition to concern over how Kristi would respond to his family, he worried that she might say or do the wrong thing at any moment simply because she was unfamiliar with Amish ways.

On second thought, it might be me who says or does the wrong thing. Joel's jaw tightened. It seemed to be the norm whenever he visited his family.

He glanced to his right and observed Kristi, noticing her head turned toward the side window, with both hands resting on her lap. Was she looking at the scenery or thinking about all the things he'd told her so far?

I shouldn't have waited so long to admit I used to be Amish, he berated himself. *It didn't do a thing to strengthen our relationship. If anything, it probably made it worse.*

Sweat beaded on Joel's forehead as he continued to mull things over. *If she knew about my other deceptions, she'd probably never talk to me again. Sure wish she hadn't gotten so quiet all of a sudden.*

Releasing one sweaty hand from the steering wheel, he rubbed it dry on his pants. Joel tried to relax, but as they approached his father's driveway, he was hit with a wave of nausea. It was hard to believe Dad was actually gone, but all the buggies parked in the field gave truth to the fact of how many people had come here today to pay their last respects and uphold Joel's family. It was the Amish way.

Joel pulled his car up beside Dad's barn and turned off the engine. Reaching across the seat, he took Kristi's hand. "Are you sure you're ready for this?"

Squeezing his fingers, she nodded.

Doris peered out the living-room window, watching as her brother got out of his car. He strode around to the other side and opened the door for another passenger. Then the two started walking toward the house. "There's a young woman with Joel. I wonder who she is." Doris turned to her sister Arlene who stood beside her, holding baby Samuel.

Arlene stepped closer to the window. "I have no idea, but her auburn hair is sure pretty. When Joel was here yesterday, he didn't say anything about bringing anyone to the funeral with him."

"Maybe she's his girlfriend. Look, he has his arm around her waist."

"Or maybe she's his *fraa*. Could Joel have gotten married without telling any of us?"

Arlene shrugged her slender shoulders. "I wouldn't put anything past our brother."

"Me neither." Doris sniffed and dabbed at her tears. "Whoever the woman is, I'm afraid she's going to see us with red-rimmed, swollen eyes. These past three days it's been hard for me not to cry every time I think of Dad."

"Same here. It's so difficult to accept his death."

Their sister, Elsie, joined them at the window. "I see our *bruder* made it. Who's the young woman walking up the stairs with him?

Do either of you recognize her?"

Arlene shook her head.

Doris turned her hands palm up. "I don't know. Let's open the door and find out."

CHAPTER 3

As Kristi stood beside Joel at his father's graveside service, she observed those around them. Everyone wore somber expressions, and the four girls, whom she'd learned were Elsie and Arlene's daughters, wept openly. Kristi had a difficult time, herself, as she swallowed around the lump in her throat. She thought about how Joel and his family must feel right now. Since she hadn't met any of them until today, Kristi could only try to put herself in their shoes.

She'd always been emotional when it came to these types of situations. Even when it was a joyous occasion, she could cry at the drop of a hat. Whenever Kristi heard "Taps" or a sentimental song on the radio, her eyes would well up with tears. As soon as she heard the "Wedding March" in a marriage scene in a movie, her tears flowed. But right now, Kristi wanted to be strong for Joel.

Taking a deep breath, she fought for control and reached for Joel's hand—not only to give herself comfort, but to offer him reassurance, as well. She glanced at him, unable to read his stoic expression. Throughout the funeral service held in his father's home,

Joel hadn't shed a single tear. Nor had he cried when the family filed up to the coffin to view the deceased's body. Even on the night Joel learned of his father's death, he had shown little emotion—at least not in Kristi's presence. Perhaps he had done his crying privately or yesterday at the viewing. She hoped it was the case, because holding one's feelings in was not a good thing.

While Kristi never had the opportunity to meet Eustace Byler, her heart went out to his family as they huddled together. Joel had been right when he'd told her what to expect today. This was not the typical funeral she'd attended in the past.

A slight wind blew, scattering golden leaves across the cemetery and filling the air with a damp, musty aroma. Dismal gray clouds covered the sky, but at least it wasn't raining. In the distance, Kristi noticed a tree giving off hints of an autumn blush. It stood vivid against the drab, colorless sky.

Turning her head to the left, Kristi noticed a young woman with golden-brown hair glance in her direction, then look quickly away. Was she part of Joel's family—someone she hadn't met? Or perhaps she was a member of Joel's father's church. The woman appeared to be around Joel's age. She was pretty, even though her blue eyes were puffy from crying. It appeared the young woman had come alone, for she stood off to one side by herself.

Since Joel and Kristi were the only people dressed in English clothes, others were probably curious about them. Of course, many of them knew Joel personally. But since he'd left the Amish faith so many years ago, some might not realize who he was.

Before long, the four pallbearers, each bearing a shovel, began taking dirt from the pile near the grave and covering up the coffin. While the grave was being filled in, a men's group sang a hymn. Without the aid of any instruments, their voices filled the air with the sobering music. Once again, Kristi had to blink rapidly in an attempt to keep her eyes dry. At the conclusion of the graveside service, the bishop asked the people to pray the Lord's Prayer silently.

"I'm expected to go back to the house now for a meal and to visit awhile," Joel whispered to Kristi. "Are you okay with it?"

She gave an affirmative nod. In addition to doing the right thing, she was eager to become more familiar with Joel's family. Those Kristi had been introduced to so far seemed kind. How could Joel keep from mentioning such a wonderful family to her all this time?

After the simple funeral dinner, many people lingered. While Joel was outside visiting, Kristi went into the house to talk to his sisters.

"What a beautiful piece. Did someone in your family make it?" Kristi asked Doris, when she noticed a lovely blue-and-pink quilted wall hanging with a star-pattern draped across the back of the couch.

Doris's eyes mirrored an inner glow as she trailed her fingers over the material. "My mother made it. She was always making full-sized quilts, wall hangings, table runners, and even potholders. Mama gave quilts to each of her daughters, as well as to many of her friends in the area."

"I'm impressed. She did beautiful work."

"I agree. My sister Elsie's hobby is needle-point." Doris motioned to the wall across the room. "See the wall hanging there with the two hummingbirds and flowers? She made it for Mama as a Christmas gift one year."

"Your sister does nice work." Kristi moved closer to take a better look. "I'm sure it takes a lot of patience to finish such a project."

"Actually, Elsie says she finds it quite relaxing to sit and needlepoint. She's spent many hours making special items for family members and friends." Doris smiled. "We all enjoy doing things meaningful with our hands during the long hours of winter." She moved over to the couch and lifted the quilted wall hanging into her arms. "I'm surprised Dad kept all the quilts she didn't give away, but then he had a hard time parting with anything. Some have called him a hoarder, and I guess it's true."

Kristi reached out to touch the wall hanging, gently tracing her fingers on the stitches. "It was thoughtful of your mother to make something so lovely, especially for her children." She sighed. "Someday, after Joel and I are married, I hope to own a quilt. Even a small one like this would be nice."

"Are you and my brother engaged?" Doris questioned.

Kristi nodded. "Well, not officially. I don't have a ring yet, but he did propose, and my answer was yes."

"Then you'll soon be part of our family." Doris handed Kristi the quilt. "Since you will become Joel's wife, I'd like you to have one of Mama's wall hangings. I'm sure my sisters would agree."

"I saw some Amish-made quilts in a shop in Berlin, and they were expensive. How much would you charge?" Simply holding the quilted piece gave Kristi a warm feeling.

"Oh, my, not a penny. It's a gift from our family." Doris clasped Kristi's arm. "You can either take this or choose one from some others in a box under my folks' bed."

"I'd like this one." Kristi fingered the edge of the quilt. She couldn't believe she'd been presented with such a special gift. "I'll take good care of it. Thank you so much." She laid it down and gave Doris a hug.

"You're more than welcome. Before you go home, I'll put it in a plastic bag so it doesn't get dirty." Doris placed her hands on the back of the couch. "Now I have a favor to ask."

"Anything. Anything at all."

"I was wondering, if you have any influence over Joel, could you ask him to come visit more often?"

"Doesn't he do it now?"

"He rarely comes around, and when he does. . ." Doris's voice trailed off.

"Joel works long hours because of his business. There are times when we've had plans to do something together, and he ends up working instead." Kristi didn't know why she felt the need to defend Joel. Working long hours was hardly an excuse for neglecting his family. "I'm sorry. I'll have a talk with Joel about coming to visit more often." Kristi took out a pen and tablet from her purse. Then she wrote down her phone number and handed it to Doris. "If there's ever a time you can't reach Joel, please give me a call."

"I appreciate it. I'll give you my number, too." After Doris wrote her phone number down for Kristi, she gestured to the kitchen. "Why don't we go find Elsie and Arlene? I'd like them to get to know you better, too."

◦───◦

As Joel wandered around the yard, trying to avoid certain people, he glanced toward the back of Dad's property. The tree house had been destroyed, but the heavily damaged section of the tree showed Joel where it had been. All that was left of the tree house were a few pieces of burned wood in a heap at the bottom of the tree. Even the steps, still nailed to the trunk, had been charred and blackened by the force of the lightning.

Joel stopped and stared at the giant maple. From the blown-away bark at the top of the tree, the lightning had made a visible path all the way down its trunk. Some long pieces of splintered maple lay scattered on the ground a few feet from the tree. Other fragments of wood clung to the trunk, curled back like a banana peel.

Stubborn man. Joel grunted. *Can't figure*

out why he'd want to build a tree house. Going up there with a storm approaching was a dumb idea.

He leaned against a fence post, reflecting on his childhood. He and Doris had spent many hours playing hide-and-seek in Dad's barn. They'd also climbed trees, taken turns on the swing, and chased after the cats. *Wish Dad would have built a tree house when I was a boy. I could have had a lot of fun playing in it and maybe even camped out during the hot summer months.*

Joel glanced to the top of the hill that overlooked his parents' farm. It wasn't as exciting as a tree house, but at least he'd had a special place up there. It was too late for any of that, though. Joel's childhood was over, and Dad was gone.

Joel watched as his aunt Verna visited on the porch with Arlene's two girls, Martha and Lillian. She was showing them how to master some techniques with a yo-yo. It was typical of Aunt Verna. She'd always had a way with children, even though she'd never had any of her own. Her yearning for children may have drawn her to them. Joel remembered one time when Aunt Verna came to his tenth birthday party and brought him a big jar of marbles. Joel had never expressed a desire to have a marble collection, but watching Aunt Verna get down on her knees to compete with him in a game of marbles got his attention. Surprisingly enough, she was good at it. Joel wondered if Aunt Verna and Dad had played with those same marbles when they were children. Although Joel's aunt wasn't a hoarder, like Dad, she did enjoy a few collections. Joel had to admit he liked to hang on to some things, himself. He'd even kept those marbles from long ago and had packed them away in one of his closets.

Glancing at his watch, Joel started for the house to find Kristi. He figured she was visiting with his sisters and could only imagine what they might be talking about.

Wouldn't be surprised if I'm the topic of their conversation. Sure hope no one has said anything negative about me.

Joel had only made it halfway there when he spotted his ex-girlfriend, Anna Detweiler, heading in his direction. His heart raced as she came closer. *Oh, great. I wonder what she wants. If Kristi sees me talking to her, how will I explain? Anna is the last person I want to speak to right now.*

CHAPTER 4

Joel was almost to the porch when Anna stepped up to him. "Hello, Joel."

He paused and turned to look at her, sweat trailing down his forehead. "Oh, hey Anna."

"I—I wanted to say I'm sorry for your loss." Anna's smile quivered. "I also wanted to let you know I'll be praying for your family."

Joel noticed Anna was fidgeting with her hands and realized that the situation was as awkward for her as it was him, but he couldn't be rude. "Thanks, Anna. I appreciate your concern." He shuffled his feet a few times. It felt strange speaking to her after all these years. Anna had matured and was as pretty as ever. With golden brown hair peeking out from her head covering and clear blue eyes, she was stunning. He noticed the pill-sized mole on her neck. "Uh, so how are you these days?" he stammered.

With her gaze fixed on him, Anna answered, "I'm doing all right. How about you?"

Joel wasn't about to admit his life was a train wreck, so he forced a smile and lifted his shoulders in a brief shrug. "I'm doin' great. I have my own business, and it keeps me plenty busy. What about you? Are you still teaching at the school in Farmerstown?"

She nodded. "Unless I get married someday, I'll probably keep on teaching."

"I'll bet my nieces and nephews enjoy having you as their teacher."

"I enjoy them, too." Anna's face turned pink. "Did you hear that my folks moved to Indiana?"

He shook his head. "Why'd they move?"

"They wanted to be close to my sister Nancy. She recently had a baby."

"I'm surprised you didn't go with them."

Her cheek color deepened. "I like my job and the area here."

"Oh, I see." Joel shoved his hands into his jacket pockets. He was tempted to ask if Anna had a suitor but thought better of it. It wasn't his business, and she might think he had regrets about breaking up with her.

"Who's the auburn-haired woman who came with you today? Is she your wife?"

Anna's question caused Joel to stumble back a step. "What? Uh, no, but Kristi and I are planning to be married. We haven't picked a date yet."

Anna lowered her gaze. "Well, she's beautiful."

"Yes. Yes, she is. However, Kristi's beauty

WANDA E. BRUNSTETTER & JEAN BRUNSTETTER

is more than skin-deep." Joel slid his hands out of his pockets and fiddled with his shirt collar. "She's the most amazing woman I've ever met."

Anna lifted her gaze to meet his again and blinked several times. "You once told me the same thing."

A surge of heat shot up the back of Joel's neck and spread quickly to his face. His body felt like it was encased in concrete. Anna was right, of course. When they had been courting, he'd often told her how special she was. Back then, she was everything to him. But things changed once Joel made the decision to leave the Amish faith.

Unsure of how to respond to Anna's statement or whether he should say anything at all, Joel awkwardly touched the side of her elbow. "It's been nice seeing you again, but I'd better go check on Kristi." Without waiting for Anna's response, he hurried up the stairs onto the porch. He was about to open the door when a hand rested on his shoulder. He twisted his head to see who had touched him.

"Well, for goodness' sake. If it isn't my favorite nephew." Aunt Verna held out her arms and gave him a hug.

He patted her back tenderly. "Nice to see

you, too." As Joel hugged his aunt, he couldn't help noticing how abruptly Anna turned and headed toward the backyard.

"I missed seeing you the last time I was here, but Elsie explained you were busy with work and couldn't come for a visit." Aunt Verna motioned for them to take a seat in two empty chairs on the porch.

When Joel sat down to face her, he noticed her sorrowful expression. He felt bad seeing his aunt like this, but he couldn't tell her that he'd missed seeing her during her last visit because his dad wouldn't appreciate his presence. After the last encounter they'd had, Joel was sure his dad never wanted to see him again. *I needed money from Dad.* Joel pinned his arms against his stomach. *Sure wish things had played out differently. Maybe I shouldn't have gotten so irritated with him. But he was the one who got mad first, and for no good reason.*

"I'm sorry I couldn't be here then, but it's good to see you now, Aunt Verna." He reached over and patted her hand.

"I know. I only wish it could be under more pleasant circumstances." She sniffed and dabbed at the tears on her wrinkled cheeks. "I'm gonna miss your daed so much. He was the best bruder. We always had such fun together."

Joel listened while his aunt reminisced about some of the things she and Dad had done while growing up. Then she told him about her last visit and how excited Dad had been when he was building the tree house. "He did it in memory of your mamm." Tears trickled down her cheeks as she spoke. "Eustace told me Effie had always wanted a tree house."

"Really? I didn't realize that." He raised his eyebrows. "I don't recall it ever being mentioned when I was a boy."

Aunt Verna shook her head. "I don't think Effie brought it up till you were grown and had left the Amish faith."

"Oh, I see. After all these years, guess there's a lot I don't know." Joel glanced at the house, wondering why Kristi hadn't come out. She'd been in there quite a while.

Kristi stood at the kitchen window, watching Joel visit with an elderly woman. But that wasn't what had initially drawn her attention to the window. She'd seen him talking to the young Amish woman she'd noticed during the graveside service. Kristi wondered, yet again, about the woman and was tempted to ask one of Joel's sisters who she was, but she didn't want to appear nosey. Kristi felt vulnerable being around so many people she didn't know and who spoke a different language when they conversed with one another. Thankfully, Joel's sisters were warm and friendly and had made her feel welcome. She felt drawn to their quiet demeanor and plain lifestyle. Kristi wondered what it would be like to live a simpler life without the distractions of TV, computers, and cell phones. Not that those things were bad. But most people seemed to focus on electronic gadgets instead of concentrating on developing good relationships with others. Kristi wasn't sure she could give up all her modern conveniences, but she longed for an unpretentious way of life.

"We believe in putting God first, and our family second," Doris had told Kristi a few minutes ago, when she'd commented on the caring attitude she'd sensed in the people who had come to the funeral.

Earlier, Kristi had noticed an older man who had his dog with him. When she and Joel ended up sitting on the same bench in the yard after their meal, he'd introduced himself as Eustace's good friend Henry. He was a real gentleman and even introduced his dog. It seemed strange that someone would bring a dog to this somber occasion, but Henry had kept Peaches in her cage until they'd eaten. Kristi thought the dog was cute, and the cocker spaniel seemed to like her. While Kristi had listened to Henry talk, Peaches had curled up beside her feet. Kristi could tell Henry hurt from losing his best friend, and he'd recalled nothing but good things about Eustace. Henry even had Kristi laughing at times, which felt good on this sobering day. No wonder he'd been Eustace's good friend.

After talking with Henry, and hearing Arlene mention how many people helped set things up for the service, as well as the meal, was it any wonder these people were so closely knit? Helping out during times of need seemed to be a normal occurrence among the Amish. *We English could learn a lesson from them*, Kristi thought.

A light tap on her arm caused Kristi to turn away from the window. She'd been so caught up in her thoughts she hadn't realized Elsie stood beside her.

"You look tired." Elsie slipped her arm around Kristi's waist.

Kristi nodded, stifling a yawn. "I am a bit. It's been a long day. Joel and I got up early so we could be here on time."

"Would you like to lie down in the guest

room awhile?" Arlene offered.

"No. Thank you, though. Joel will probably want to go soon anyway."

"How about another cup of coffee or a piece of zucchini bread?" Doris motioned to the desserts sitting out on the table. "Feel free to help yourself to anything you like. It looks like there will be lots of leftover chocolate-chip cookies. I'll get some for you to take home so you and Joel can share." Doris opened the container on the counter.

Kristi watched her put a paper plate into the bag before placing the treats inside. She'd already sampled one of the soft, chewy cookies and found them to be quite tasty. She was on the verge of pouring a cup of coffee when Joel stepped into the room. "Kristi and I should go, but first I need to ask you a question, Elsie."

"What is it, Joel?" She looked at him curiously.

"Where's Dad's will? We need to find out how much he left us."

Kristi couldn't believe Joel would bring up this topic on the day of his father's funeral when the pain of losing him was so raw. She felt embarrassed. The last thing Joel should be concerned with right now was his father's will. And why had he been avoiding his family? What was wrong with him, anyway?

"Listen, Joel." Elsie's chin quivered as she looked at him with watery eyes. "This is not the time to be discussing Dad's will. We can talk about it in a week or so, once things have settled down for all of us."

"That's right," Arlene agreed.

Joel's eyes narrowed into tiny slits. "We don't have to discuss the will right now. I just want to know where it is."

"We don't want to discuss this today." Doris spoke up.

"Well, I do!" Joel shouted.

"I couldn't help overhearing you talking from the other room, and there's no need for knowing right now," Elsie's husband, John, intervened as he entered the kitchen.

Kristi held her breath, watching Joel's ears turn pink and waiting to hear his response.

Joel strode across the room until he was mere inches from John. The men were about the same height, so they were eye-to-eye and practically nose-to-nose. Kristi feared Joel might be about to punch Elsie's husband. "Listen to me, John, this is between me and my sisters, so I'd appreciate it if you'd just stay out of it and mind your own business."

John's face colored, too, and his brown

eyes narrowed through his glasses. "Whatever involves my fraa is my business, plain and simple. Furthermore, if you were truly interested in a relationship with your family, you'd come around more often, and without always asking for money. It seems now you are concerned about money again, or you wouldn't be worried about Eustace's will."

"I'm not worried. I'd just like to know—"

John held up his hand. "We don't want any trouble here today. Our family is under enough sorrow and strain."

The room got deathly quiet. Kristi was sure if a feather floated from the sky, she would hear it drop. These last few minutes, watching her fiancé's expression and listening to the anger in his voice, gave a pretty clear picture of why he hadn't previously told her about his Amish family. He obviously did not get along with them, and for good reason. From what she'd heard here in this kitchen, the man she loved and hoped to marry cared more about money than he did his own family. Didn't Joel feel remorse that his father had been killed less than a week ago? Wasn't he grieving like his siblings were? She clenched her teeth. *Maybe I don't know Joel as well as I thought.*

Joel whirled around, his dark brown eyes

blazing as he looked at Kristi. "You'd better gather up your things. We're leaving!" He turned and pointed his finger at Elsie. "I'll call you in a few days to talk about Dad's will."

CHAPTER 5

The first thirty minutes on the road, Joel remained quiet. Kristi did, too. She needed time to process everything—especially the scene when Joel had asked about his father's will. *More like demanded,* she thought, glancing at Joel and noting his smooth, expressionless features. Kristi still couldn't believe the scene she had witnessed. Everyone in the room had looked like codfish, the way their jaws dropped open. *How could Joel be so insensitive? Or had he spoken in frustration from grief over losing his father? If so, how can I help Joel or support him when he needs it? He seems to keep things bottled up most of the time.*

Earlier, Kristi had wondered how she would be accepted by Joel's family. She'd hoped they would all like her and had felt comfortable with his sisters, but things had been awkward after Joel's confrontation with his brother-in-law.

Unable to bear the silence any longer, Kristi reached across the seat and touched Joel's arm. "Mind if I ask you a question?"

"Sure, ask me anything you want." His gaze remained fixed on the road.

"Who was the Amish woman you were talking to in the yard before you came in the house to get me?"

"Which Amish woman? I talked to a lot of people today."

"The younger one with golden-brown hair. You talked to her for a while, before you stepped onto the porch and began a conversation with an older woman."

"The older woman is my aunt Verna. She's Dad's only sibling."

Kristi sighed as she nudged Joel's arm. "Okay, but she's not the woman I was asking about, Joel. It's the younger one."

"Uh. . . Her name is Anna Detweiler."

"Is she a relative?"

"No, she's not."

"Then a friend, perhaps?"

"Yeah, I guess." A muscle on the side of Joel's neck quivered.

"Is there something you're not telling me? Is Anna more than a friend?"

He turned his head and frowned. "What's with the twenty questions?"

"I haven't asked you twenty questions. I simply want to know about Anna Detweiler."

"She was my girlfriend. We were engaged to be married." Joel glanced out his side window, then back to the road again, avoiding her stare. "Satisfied?"

Kristi flinched, as if he'd thrown a glass of cold water in her face. She wasn't about to let this matter drop. "No, I am not satisfied, and I don't appreciate the tone of voice you're using."

He let go of the steering wheel and clasped her hand. "Sorry, Kristi. I'm not myself today."

Although it was a considerate gesture, his touch felt unsympathetic. Usually, Kristi would wrap her fingers around Joel's, but her hand rested lifeless in his grasp. "I can't argue with you there. I'm not even sure who the real Joel is anymore."

"Can't you understand, Kristi? I'm stressed out. I've got a lot on my plate, trying to run a business. Now with my dad dying and my sisters refusing to talk about his will, I'm very upset."

"I do understand, but as your brother-in-law mentioned, today was not the best time to discuss the will."

Joel let go of Kristi's hand. "Didn't you hear what I told Elsie before we left? I ended the matter by telling her I'd call her in a few days to talk about it."

"Yes, I heard, but what I'm wondering is why it's so important to you. Are you expecting a big inheritance?"

Joel bobbed his head. "My dad was a millionaire, Kristi. There are oil wells on the back of his property."

"Really? Guess I didn't notice."

"That's because you never saw what's out back. I'm sure he has more money in the bank than most Amish people see in a lifetime."

She tugged on the end of her jacket while shaking her head. "Money isn't everything, Joel."

"It is to me."

Kristi rubbed her forehead to ward off the headache she felt coming on. Were Joel's business struggles making him desperate for money? Even if they were, he needed to take time to grieve the loss of his father, not worry about the will. She'd heard her pastor say on more than one occasion how sad it was when someone died and the family fought over who would get what. It was not the Christian thing to do and did nothing to cement a family's relationship. People needed to bind together during difficult times, not worry about their selfish ambitions.

"Let's talk about something else, shall we?" Joel maneuvered his car into the right-hand lane. "I don't want to discuss this the whole way home."

Figuring it would be best to comply,

Kristi pointed to the plastic bags by her feet. "Before I tell you what's in the bigger bag, Arlene gave us some chocolate-chip cookies in the smaller bag."

"That's nice. I'm sure they'll be good."

"And best of all. . ." Kristi pointed to the larger bag. "Doris gave me one of your mother's beautiful quilted wall hangings."

"Did she?"

Kristi opened the bag and pulled out one edge of the quilt so he could see the pattern and pretty colors. She didn't want to risk getting it dirty if it touched the floor. "Yes. When I admired this and she found out I was your fiancée—"

"You told her?" Joel's mouth twitched as he glanced her way.

"I figured she already knew." Kristi's spine stiffened. "Why didn't you tell your family about me, Joel?" She folded the edge of the wall hanging so it was safely tucked inside the bag.

"I would have—eventually." He looked back at the road.

"When? Would you have waited till we were married? After we had kids?" Her voice choked with tears, Kristi tugged at her jacket collar. "Would you have ever told them?"

His shoulders slumped. "Of course I was

gonna tell them. I was simply waiting for the right time."

"Why did there have to be a right time?" Kristi was beyond frustrated. "Your sisters were so kind and welcoming. I would have liked to have become acquainted with them from the time we started dating." Her tone softened.

"Sorry, I thought...." He lifted one hand. "Oh, what does it matter? I can't change the past. We need to focus on our future."

Do we have a future? Kristi wondered, but she didn't voice her question. Now wasn't the time for them to get into a heated debate about this—especially since she wasn't composed enough to reason with him.

Kristi observed Joel as he kept driving. She couldn't begin to imagine what was going through his head. Yes, she was upset that he'd kept his heritage from her, but he had just lost his father. Kristi poked her tongue on the inside of her cheek. Was it fair to be irritated with him when he had so much on his shoulders right now? Joel needed a few days to work through the initial shock and grief over losing his father.

Charm

"I can't believe the nerve of our bruder." Arlene looked at Elsie and shook her head. "His insensitivity must have been embarrassing for Kristi. She seems like a sweet woman. I can only imagine what she thinks of our family."

"Hopefully Kristi only thinks good thoughts. When she brought up the fact that she and Joel were planning to get married, I gave her one of Mama's quilted wall hangings. It's the one that was on the back of the couch." Doris rested her hands on the back of a chair. "Kristi was admiring it, and she seemed quite happy when I gave it to her."

"I'm glad you did. She got along well with everyone today," Arlene commented. "I doubt she has any ill feelings toward us, but it makes me wonder why she got involved with Joel. He can be such a *schtinker* sometimes."

"You took the words right out of my mouth." Elsie motioned to the leftover desserts on the counter. "Joel and Kristi left in such a hurry I'm surprised you were able to get her to take the cookies before they went out the door."

Frowning, Doris leaned against the kitchen sink with her arms folded. She probably knew Joel better than any of them, and yet she couldn't figure him out. Just when, and why, had he become so desperate for money? Joel had his own business and should have been doing well with it by now. If he'd remained Amish and kept working with Dad, things would be better for everyone. Joel would be married to Anna, and maybe they'd have one or two children already. Instead, he was engaged to an English woman they knew little or nothing about. Even if Joel came around more often after they were married, Kristi would probably never fully understand the Amish way of life and might never fit in. But it would be best not to overthink things right now. It was better to take one day at a time. Perhaps everything would work out in the end.

"I wonder if Dad even made a will." Arlene's statement pushed Doris's thoughts aside.

"I'm sure he did," Elsie responded. "Once things have settled down a bit, we'll look for it." She walked over to the cups and saucers still left in the sink. "At the moment, we have more dishes to do."

"While you two work on those, I'll take the paper trash out to burn." Doris scooped up two bags and headed behind the barn, where the burn barrel was located.

*

After Doris lit a match to light the paper in the barrel, she made sure the flames took hold. She'd stay here until the fire turned to embers, to make sure it was safely out.

Doris turned her attention to the maple, where the remains of the tree house still clung. She could hardly look in the direction of the tree and tried to rethink the event, to tone down the harshness of Dad's death. *At least he died here at home and in a place he was happy.*

Not everyone agreed with Dad building the tree house, but how could one deny his happiness? Dad's face had lit up each time he announced he was doing it for their mother.

Gazing heavenward, Doris imagined her parents walking hand-in-hand. *Mama and Dad had a special bond, and now they're together.*

As she looked closer at the wood scattered around the maple, Doris saw the sun reflect on something. It looked like a piece of metal lying among the splintered wood. She glanced in the barrel and stirred up the contents. Since the flames were at a low burn, Doris thought it was safe to go see what was there.

She picked up a board, then another, and discovered birdhouses attached to each one. While the wood they were nailed to was blackened from the force of the lightning, somehow the two birdhouses remained untouched.

I'll bet, for Mama's sake, Dad nailed these to the railing of the tree house. Doris remembered fondly how much her mother loved the birds. She looked at the small-framed houses, so meticulously made by her father. The tiny perch at the opening, the imitation windows with cute little shutters on both sides, and the tin roof to keep the baby birds dry showed the love Dad had for his wife and for the birds she'd cared so much about.

Doris walked through the debris, making sure nothing else was hidden under the pieces of wood. Then she spied her dad's tool box. Incredibly, beside the open box, Doris found a third little house. It was as cute and undamaged as the first two, only shaped a bit differently. How it happened, she would never understand, since the toolbox and bird-house were only a few feet from the tree.

Doris gathered the birdhouses and put them in the small wagon Dad had often used to carry supplies. In some ways, maybe these birdhouses would bring a bit of peace to her, as well as to Arlene and Elsie.

Doris stopped at the burn barrel to check it again. She was glad the paper products burned quickly, as she was anxious to take what she'd found back to her sisters. She stirred the ashes to make sure the fire was out and was satisfied when no more smoke wisped up.

Putting the lid back on the barrel, Doris

pulled the wagon around the barn. When she came to the front, she heard a noise coming from inside and halted. She noticed the barn door slightly ajar. Was it the colt's whinny, a cat's meow, or something else she'd heard? Tilting her head to one side, Doris leaned forward and listened. It sounded like someone crying.

She dropped the handle of the wagon and slowly entered the barn. Doris let her eyes adjust to the dimness, with only the light coming through the windows. Slowly, she followed the soul-wrenching sobs. Hearing it made tears come to her eyes. *Who is in so much pain?*

As she rounded a stack of hay, Doris's hands flew to her mouth. Lying on a bed of straw in an empty horse stall was Anna.

She ran quickly to her friend's side, crouched down, and held Anna in her arms. "Are you okay? I thought you'd already left."

Sniffling and choking on sobs, Anna sat up. "I shouldn't be blubbering like a *boppli*, but seeing Joel today with his fiancée upset me. I thought I'd gotten over him, but my feelings for Joel are still here." Anna placed one hand against her heart. "I've kept them buried."

Using the corner of her apron, Doris dried Anna's tear-stained cheeks. Anna was a good person, and she hated to see her suffer this way.

❧

Akron

After Joel dropped Kristi off at her condo that evening, he went straight home and got out the Corvette. Today had been stressful, and he needed some time alone. A few hours on the open road in his shiny black Vette might be what Joel needed to ease some of his tension.

He headed down the driveway and turned onto the highway with his high-beams on, always on the lookout for deer. The last thing he needed was to hit one of them tonight and total his priceless classic, not to mention hurt a deer.

Today didn't go well with Kristi, Joel thought. *She thinks it was terrible I brought up Dad's will. If she realized how badly I need money, maybe she'd understand. But if I tell her I'm in debt up to my neck because I spent big bucks on a fancy car, she'll be even more upset.* He gripped the steering wheel and bit his lower lip. *Not to mention how angry she'd be if she found out I took money from our joint account without her knowledge.*

Joel felt like he was walking a tightrope

with no net under him. One wrong move and he could lose his balance, falling straight to his death.

I've got to find out soon if Dad has a will, and if so, how much of his money I'm entitled to. I'll wait till the middle of next week, and then I'm calling Elsie. If Dad left each of us a fourth of his assets, my sisters and I will have all the money we need. And I, for one, need it bad.

CHAPTER 6

"Y ou look tired, honey. Did you and Joel get back from his father's funeral late last night?" Kristi's mother asked when Kristi stopped by the following morning on her way to work. She was working Saturday to complete the trade she'd made with a co-worker so she could go to the funeral.

"Not too late. I'm tired because I didn't get much sleep." Kristi went over to the coffee pot and poured herself a cup, making sure it didn't overflow. After refilling the water reservoir on her parents' coffeemaker, she picked up her mug and took a seat at the kitchen table. "I stopped by to give you a treat and fill you in on a few things." She placed a bag of chocolate-chip cookies on the table. "One of Joel's sisters sent these home with us yesterday, and I wanted to share some with you."

Mom sat across from Kristi. "That was thoughtful. So why didn't you get much sleep last night?"

Kristi sighed. "Because I was, and still am, deeply troubled." When she'd learned about the death of Joel's father, Kristi had called her parents to let them know she would be traveling to the funeral with Joel.

"About Joel?" Mom took a cookie and also a napkin.

"Yes." Kristi's stomach tensed as she explained about Joel's Amish background.

"How long have you known this, Kristi?"

"I didn't know anything until yesterday. As we were driving to his dad's place in Charm, where the funeral was held, Joel blurted out his family was Amish. And get this—Joel left the faith seven years ago."

"Oh my!" Mom touched her parted lips. She seemed at a loss for words.

"I don't have anything against his Amish heritage, but I was hurt by his deception."

"And well you should be. Given all this time you've been dating Joel, he should have told you about his family long before now." Mom's gaze flicked upward. "I've always thought it a bit strange that he'd never introduced you to his family. It's not normal, Kristi. Not in a healthy, loving relationship."

Staring into her coffee cup, Kristi could only nod.

"Did you feel out of place at the funeral?"

"A little." Kristi brought her mug to her lips, but the coffee seemed to lack any taste when the warm liquid touched her tongue.

"Was Joel's family accepting of you?"

"They seemed to be. His sister Doris gave me one of her mother's quilted wall hangings." Kristi smiled. "It's so beautiful, Mom. I can't wait for you to see it."

"Oh, how nice. Was Mrs. Byler okay with her daughter giving away one of her quilts?"

"Joel's mother is also deceased."

"How sad. Does Joel have any other brothers or sisters?" Mom asked.

"Besides Doris, he has two other sisters. Joel's the youngest. Doris, Elsie, and Arlene all seemed so nice. I'm looking forward to knowing them better." Kristi wiped her mouth on a napkin and rested her elbows on the table. "I felt a sense of peace when I was with them—at least, I did until Joel caused some tension."

Mom's eyes blinked rapidly. "What happened?"

Kristi recounted the details of what had transpired when Joel asked about his father's will. "It was so embarrassing. I couldn't believe he would be insensitive enough to bring it up on the day of his dad's funeral, when everyone was grieving."

Mom's mouth opened, as though about to respond, but she allowed Kristi to keep talking.

"What's more puzzling is he didn't shed

a single tear during the funeral or graveside service."

Mom placed her hand gently on Kristi's arm. "It sounds like Joel has some serious issues he needs to deal with, Kristi. Do you see now why I've been concerned about your relationship?"

"I understand, but—"

"He's been keeping things from you, and that's never good. It's a shame Joel didn't attend the marriage seminar with you. If he'd heard what our speaker taught us, he might realize the importance of honesty between a couple." Mom leaned slightly forward. "For that matter, we should be honest with everyone. It's the Christian way. But since I'm not sure Joel is a Christian. . ."

"I'm sorry to interrupt, but I need to go." Kristi glanced at the clock on the wall. "I don't want to be late for work." A tingly sensation shot up Kristi's spine as she pushed her chair aside and stood. She said a quick goodbye to Mom and hurried out the door.

As she stood on the porch, rubbing her temples, Kristi wished she hadn't told her mother Joel had asked about his father's will—although she couldn't keep the truth about his Amish heritage from her folks. *If I hadn't told Mom about Joel's family being*

Amish, she would have fainted in shock when she saw them at our wedding. Dad may have been surprised, too. No, she'd done the right thing sharing with Mom about Joel's family being Amish. But she wished she had kept quiet about what went on after the funeral dinner.

I'll give Joel a little more time to work through things, Kristi told herself as she got in the car and headed to work. *But I'm not giving up on him, no matter what Mom thinks.*

❧

Charm

Doris's boss had given her a week off to deal with the funeral and other issues, so despite exhaustion and queasiness, Doris had gotten up early to help her sisters clean their dad's place. She'd just walked her horse into the corral and closed the latch when she heard Aunt Verna and Uncle Lester in the barn.

"Now, Lester, don't overdo. You could hurt yourself bending too far and end up straining your back."

"Aw, Verna, you worry too much. The horses' stalls need to be cleaned, and someone has to do it."

"Speak up, Lester. You're mumbling."

Uncle Lester repeated himself.

"It can wait till one of the younger men or

boys comes over," she retorted.

"Are you sayin' I'm old?"

"I didn't say anything about you being cold."

"*Old*, not *cold*." His voice rose. "You should quit being so stubborn and get a hearing aide."

"*Guder mariye*, Aunt Verna and Uncle Lester." Doris entered the barn.

"Morning, Doris," they answered in unison. Aunt Verna gave her a hug.

"I'll help you clean the stalls, as well as feed and water the horses, Uncle Lester." Doris rubbed the mane of Dad's buggy horse. It saddened her to think he would never drive this horse again.

"It's nice of you to offer." Uncle Lester leaned on his pitchfork. "I still need to let the mare and her colt out to run."

"I'll take care of it before I begin cleaning," Doris offered. "We'll get this work done in no time at all."

"Would you like a cup of coffee, Doris?" Aunt Verna plucked a piece of hay off her dress.

Doris nodded. "Jah, please."

"What did you say, dear?"

"She said 'jah.' And would you bring me a cup, too?" Uncle Lester spoke loudly.

"Okay, will do." Aunt Verna shuffled out of the barn.

Doris wondered if her aunt's hearing was steadily getting worse. She could see Uncle Lester working as hard as he could, but he moved a bit slow, no doubt due to the pain and stiffness caused by his arthritis. Doris hoped Elsie and Arlene would arrive soon to help with things in the house.

A short time later, a rig pulled into the yard. Doris ran out and waved at Elsie.

Uncle Lester stuck his head out to check what was happening. "I see your sister's here." His brows furrowed. "I wonder where our coffee is."

"I bet Aunt Verna got sidetracked." Doris watched Elsie unhitch her horse and take him to the corral. When she finished, they walked together to the barn.

"How's it going?" Elsie asked.

"We're cleaning the horses' stalls, but we could sure use some coffee." Uncle Lester grunted. "Don't know what your aunt's up to. Would you go in and remind her that we're still waiting?"

Elsie nodded. "I'll get your coffees. Maybe Aunt Verna is busy with something."

When Elsie returned a few minutes later holding cups of steaming coffee, she smiled and said, "Aunt Verna was sitting in the living room, reading. I didn't mean to, but I made her jump, because she hadn't heard me come in. I gave her a hug and then mentioned the coffee."

"What'd she say?" Uncle Lester cocked his head.

"She forgot, so I told her to relax and enjoy her book, and I'd bring out the coffee."

Doris wasn't surprised when Elsie handed them their cups and picked up a broom. She never had been one to stand around when work needed to be done. This gave Uncle Lester a chance to sit on an old stool and drink his coffee.

Doris sipped her own coffee and set the cup on a wooden box so she could help Elsie. Soon, they had the horses taken care of and each of the stalls cleaned. When they were done and the tools had been put away, they headed for the house. "Look!" Doris pointed toward the driveway. "Here comes Arlene now."

Uncle Lester went on ahead, but Doris and Elsie waited for Arlene. Once her horse had been put away, they walked into Dad's house together. They'd gotten a lot done yesterday, cleaning up after the funeral, but it had been an exhausting day for everyone. All were in agreement to go home and get a good night's rest and return in the morning to do more. Aunt Verna and Uncle Lester would be staying at Dad's for the next few weeks to help out, but Doris and her sisters didn't expect their aunt and uncle to do everything on their own. It was their place to clean Dad's house and sort through all his things.

"Did you sleep well last night?" Arlene asked Doris while she swept the kitchen floor. "You left in such a hurry yesterday."

"No, not really. I had a troubling night. All I did was toss and turn. I'm sorry Brian and I left so quickly." Doris sighed, setting a container on the table before plopping down on a chair. "I brought some apples, oranges, grapes, and celery filled with peanut butter. What we don't eat today, we can put in the fridge, since we'll be coming back on Monday to finish cleaning and begin the sorting process."

"Seems like now's a good time to have a snack and talk a spell." Elsie found a box of crackers in the cupboard and called their aunt and uncle to join them.

Opening the refrigerator, Arlene took out a block of cheese left over from the funeral and then grabbed a knife from the counter. "Elsie, why don't you slice the apples and cheese, while I make us some hot tea?" she suggested.

Soon everyone was seated at the table.

"This sure hits the spot." Aunt Verna reached for a slice of cheese. "I think we all needed a break."

Arlene blew on her steaming cup of tea and glanced at Doris. "I was concerned when Brian rushed in and told us you were leaving yesterday. I figured the day's events might have hit you all of a sudden."

"You're right, it did, but it wasn't just the exhaustion from the funeral. I was upset by something else." Doris closed her eyes and drew a deep breath. "Even now, thinking about it, makes me feel nauseous."

"Did something happen?" Uncle Lester asked.

Doris nodded, then quickly explained how she'd discovered Anna when she was heading back from burning the trash. "I never heard such a gut-wrenching cry."

"Come to think of it, I don't remember saying goodbye to Anna yesterday." Arlene handed Doris a napkin. "Why was she crying so hard? Was it because of Joel?"

"Jah." Doris went on to say how, once Anna had calmed down, she'd confessed her love for Joel had never died. "I thought after all these years she'd gotten over him. Apparently, Anna did, too, until she came

71

face-to-face with our bruder yesterday."

"Oh dear." Elsie sighed, and Aunt Verna slowly shook her head.

"Anna said when she looked into Joel's eyes, she realized she'd buried her feelings. Then when Anna found out who Kristi was and how much Joel's girlfriend meant to him, she was devastated." Doris wiped the tears on her cheeks. "All this time Anna's been hoping Joel would return home to the Amish faith and their relationship could be rekindled. Now she feels all is lost, realizing her dreams were for nothing."

"Our brother!" Elsie grumbled. "I don't understand him at all. Joel is a different person than he was growing up. He had a good thing with Anna."

Arlene nodded. "I hardly know him anymore."

"After Anna and I finished talking, I drove her home in her buggy while Brian followed me in ours," Doris continued. "That's why we left in a hurry with no explanation."

"Poor Anna." Aunt Verna patted Doris's arm. "It's good she confided in you."

Doris nodded. "Now that I know, I want to offer her my support."

Everyone ate in silence until Doris jumped up. "I almost forgot something I want you to see. I'll be right back." She rushed out the door.

Shortly after, as Doris pulled the little wagon toward the porch, Arlene and Elsie came out.

"What do you have there?" Arlene asked.

"It's something I found yesterday up by the maple tree that was hit by lightning. Something for each of us in memory of Mama and Dad."

As Doris handed her sisters each a birdhouse, she explained how she had come upon them.

"Looks like I may need a tissue." Teary-eyed, Elsie stared at the birdhouse she'd been given. "This is so special."

"When I took the trash out to be burned and found the birdhouses unscorched by the lightning's heat, I believed it was meant to be," Doris said. "I think I was meant to find Anna, as well."

❧

Akron

When Kristi got home from work late in the afternoon, the first thing she did was call Joel. She drew a deep breath when he answered.

"Hi, Joel. How was your day?"

"Okay, I guess."

"How are you doing? Were you able to get a good night's sleep?"

"Not really, but I'm fine." Joel's tone lacked emotion.

"Why don't we work out at the gym for a while?" she suggested, hoping it might perk him up. "Afterward, we can go somewhere for a bite to eat."

"I'm too tired from work, and I don't feel like getting cleaned up to go out."

"Would you rather come here for supper? It's a bit chilly outside but not too cold to put burgers on the grill."

"Not tonight, Kristi."

Kristi winced. "Please don't shut me out, Joel. Whether you realize it or not, you need support right now."

"I'm fine, really. I just need to be alone."

"Okay, I'll let you go, but don't hesitate to call if you want to talk."

"Thanks for understanding. Maybe we can do something tomorrow."

"That'd be nice. If the weather cooperates, why don't we go on a picnic at the park after church?"

"Whatever you want to do is fine." Joel's words were positive, but the tone of his voice was not. Was he telling her what he thought she wanted to hear, or was he looking forward to being with her? She hoped it was the latter.

"Okay, I'll see you tomorrow. Have a good evening."

"You too, Kristi. Bye."

Kristi set her cell phone aside and went to the bedroom to change into her sweatpants. It wouldn't be dark for another hour or so, and she thought about going for a run. While getting dressed, however, Kristi saw her laptop lying on the bed. She stared at it a few seconds, wondering if she should go online or head out for a run. *Maybe I won't feel like an outsider if I do more Amish research.*

She picked up her laptop and carried it to the living room. *If I'm going to be part of Joel's family someday, I need to learn all I can about their way of life.*

CHAPTER 7

Millersburg

Monday morning, as soon as the children were off to school and John had left for work, Elsie slipped into her shoes and went out to the phone shack to check for messages.

Cautiously peering in to make sure no spiders lurked about, Elsie stepped inside the small wooden building. She took a seat on the folding chair and started replaying the first message.

"Hey, Elsie. It's Joel. I'm calling to see if you've located Dad's will."

Elsie's fingers curled into her palms. *I can't believe him! When does he think we would have had time to look for Dad's will? And why does he need money so bad? I have half a mind not to even call him back.*

She took in a couple of deep breaths, trying to calm herself. Joel could be so insensitive. Didn't he realize how badly they were all grieving? Wasn't he grieving the loss of their dad, too?

"Maybe not," Elsie grumbled aloud. "Our brother might only be thinking of himself.

I'll bet Joel doesn't realize how unfeeling he sounds."

Struggling with whether to call Joel or not, Elsie finally picked up the phone. She felt a release of tension when she heard Joel's voice mail play. It would be easier to leave him a message. Less chance of getting into an argument, which neither of them needed right now.

"Hello, Joel, it's Elsie returning your call. We haven't had time yet to look for Dad's will. Aunt Verna and Uncle Lester are still here. They'll be staying at Dad's house for a few weeks to help us sort through things. We'll call you if his will turns up in the process. Please try not to worry about it for now. When things settle down a bit, we'd like to have you and Kristi over for supper. Doris, Arlene, and I enjoyed meeting her. She seems nice, and we're happy she has one of Mama's quilted wall hangings. I'll get back to you in a few weeks."

Elsie placed the phone back on the receiver, letting a soft breath escape her lips. She was trying her best to be confident throughout this whole process, but she felt frail, struggling against the urge to break down and scream.

She closed her eyes. *I'm the oldest child. I have to stay strong, not only for myself but also for my sisters. Imagine how they'd feel if they saw their oldest sister acting like a scared, overly emotional child. Please help me, Lord. I can't do it without Your help.* Elsie quoted Philippians 4:13, "I can do all things through Christ which strengtheneth me."

A crawling sensation tickled her arm. Elsie opened her eyes, raised her arm, and shrieked. Feeling rather foolish, she brought her hand close to her face, eyeing a strand of long hair dangling from her fingers. Elsie chuckled slightly. She was glad it wasn't a spider.

She was about to leave the phone shack when the phone rang. Hoping it wasn't Joel, Elsie was tempted to let the answering machine pick up. But it could be someone else. "Hello," she said hesitantly.

"Hi, Elsie. It's Doris. I'm sorry I won't be able to meet you and Arlene at Dad's house today. Unfortunately, I've come down with the flu." Doris spoke softly, her voice trembling.

Elsie's forehead wrinkled. "I'm sorry to hear you're feeling poorly, but don't worry about it. We'll manage without your help today. Aunt Verna is itching to help us, since she got some much needed rest on Sunday."

"*Danki.* I appreciate it. I'm glad I have the day off and can stay home and take it easy."

"That's what you need to do, all right.

Have you taken your temperature to see if you have a fever?"

"I did, and it's normal. I don't ache anywhere, either, but I'm quite nauseous. I couldn't keep my breakfast down."

"Please get some rest and let me know if you need anything. I'll be over at Dad's helping Aunt Verna and Arlene most of the day, but I'll make sure to check Dad's answering machine in case you need us to bring you anything."

"Thanks so much. I'll talk to you later, Elsie."

As she started back to the house, Elsie felt torn. Part of her wanted to help out at Dad's, but she also wished she could go to Doris's place to check up on her. Since Brian was no doubt at work, Doris would be alone. *Of course,* Elsie reasoned, *she has no little ones to look after, and I did tell her to call if she needs anything. She'll probably be fine. I need to stop acting like a mother hen.*

When Elsie entered her house, she went to the kitchen to put a casserole together for lunch. After placing it in the oven and setting the timer, she wandered around the house, looking for something else to do. She would be heading over to Charm soon, but the thought of sorting through Dad's things nearly broke her heart.

She paused in the living room to look out the window. Her gaze came to rest on the old wagon wheel leaning against a tree in the yard. Elsie remembered the day she'd acquired the wheel. She and Dad had gone to the local farmers' market. When she'd spotted the wheel, he'd bought it for her. Then Dad found another one and bought it for Mama. *"I'll find a place to put it when I get home,"* Elsie remembered him saying.

Swiping at the tears rolling down her cheeks, she headed back to the kitchen to check on the casserole. *Maybe I'll bake the peanut butter cookie dough resting in the refrigerator for snacks this afternoon.* Elsie closed her eyes. *Lord, please help me and my family through this difficult time.*

❧

Charm

When Elsie arrived at Dad's, she noticed Arlene's rig wasn't there yet. She tied her horse to the hitching rail and carried the box with the casserole and cookies up to the house.

Uncle Lester let her in. "Guder mariye, Elsie. You're the first to arrive."

"Good morning. Arlene should be here soon, but Doris won't be coming. She has the flu and stayed home to rest."

"Sorry to hear it. I hope she feels better soon." He closed the door and headed to the living room.

Elsie carried the food to the kitchen, where she found Aunt Verna going through a drawer in Dad's old desk. "I'm glad you're here." Aunt Verna looked up and gestured to the drawer full of pens. "We certainly have our work cut out for us today."

"We sure do, but it doesn't have to all be done in a day. In fact, it's going to take a good many weeks to sort through all my daed's collections."

Her aunt nodded. "Will your sisters be coming today?"

"Arlene will be here as soon as she drops off baby Samuel at a friend's, but Doris is sick with the flu."

Aunt Verna's brows puckered. "Did you say, 'Doris is sick and doesn't have a clue?'"

Elsie bit back a chuckle. "I said she has the flu."

"Oh, what a shame. Then she needs to rest and drink plenty of fluids."

"Jah." Elsie pointed to the casserole dish she'd set on the table. "This needs to be refrigerated, but I'll take care of it as soon as I tend to my horse."

"You go ahead. I'll deal with the casserole."

"Danki." Elsie went out to her buggy and was about to unhitch her horse when her sister pulled in. "Guder mariye," she called as Arlene guided her horse up to the hitching rail. "Doris won't be joining us today."

Arlene hopped out of the rig. "Is she okay?"

"She thinks she has the flu."

"Oh, no. Is the flu bug going around?"

Elsie shrugged. "A lot of people were at the funeral on Friday, so someone may have been coming down with it."

Arlene secured her horse then reached inside the buggy and took out a box. "I brought some pickled eggs and dilled green beans." She smacked her lips. "Both are recipes from Mama, so you know they'll be tasty."

"I brought a chicken-rice casserole and some cookies. Lunch will be good, but the reason we're here today isn't." Elsie swallowed hard.

Arlene slipped her arm around Elsie's waist. "We'll get through this. We need to trust God and pray for strength."

"You're right. Now let's put our horses in the corral so we can go inside and get started." Elsie fought the lump in her throat. "There's a lot to do."

Akron

Because Kristi's shift didn't start until ten, she planned to stop at the bank on the way to work. Friday was payday, but since she'd been at the funeral that day, she had to do the banking today. She planned to put half the money she'd earned in her and Joel's joint savings account. The rest would go in her checking to pay bills and for incidentals.

As Kristi got in her car and pulled onto the street, she thought about Joel and wondered how he was doing this morning. Yesterday, he'd called to let her know he was too tired to get out of bed and go to church with her. He sounded depressed, but Kristi wasn't sure if his fatigue and mood was from working too hard or if he was emotionally drained because of his father's death. She'd been tempted to go over to Joel's place Sunday evening to check on him but thought he might need more time alone. If Kristi had lost either of her parents, she would need all the support she could get. Joel, however, tended to withdraw when faced with an unpleasant situation. Kristi had witnessed this after Joel's accident, when he'd been unable to work for a few weeks. Every evening, she'd gone over to fix his meal, but sometimes Joel hardly seemed to notice she was there.

Maybe I'll give him a few days before I try calling again, she decided. *I don't want to appear pushy or make Joel think I'm too controlling by forcing him to talk about things when he's not ready.*

By the time she pulled up to the bank, Kristi felt a little better. She was sure Joel would call when he was ready, so stressing about it would do her no good. When he decided to open up, she would be ready to listen and offer support.

Kristi got out of her car and hurried into the bank. Fortunately, no one was in line ahead of her, so she stepped up to the teller and handed her the check. "I've filled out two deposit slips," she told the middle-age woman. "The rest, I'd like in cash."

"Would you like a balance on both your accounts?"

Kristi nodded. It had been awhile since she'd asked for a balance on her and Joel's account. She was curious to see how well they were doing. If they had enough money, maybe they could set a wedding date soon.

Kristi waited until she got back in her car to look at the deposit slips. When she did, she had to do a double take. What was written there sent a chill up her back. The account she and Joel shared had less than half the money in it since the last time she'd checked. *Wait a minute. What's going on here?* She crimped the slip between her thumb and index finger. *Did Joel withdraw money from our account without telling me?*

Kristi shook her head in disbelief as she leaned heavily against the seat. She could hardly believe Joel would do such a thing. But then, lately nothing surprised her. Too bad she didn't know where he was working today, or she'd go there right now and confront him.

Looking at her watch, she saw it was impossible. Kristi barely had time to make it to the nursing home before her shift started. She would talk to Joel when she got off work. One way or another, before the day was out, Kristi would get to the bottom of this.

CHAPTER 8

Charm

"I hardly know where to start," Arlene commented as she and Elsie entered their father's bedroom.

Elsie opened the closet door and peered in. "Maybe we should begin by going through his clothes. We can see if there's anyone in our community who might have a need or give them to the Share and Care thrift shop in Berlin."

Tears welled in Elsie's eyes. "I realize we can't keep everything, but it's going to be so hard to part with any of Dad's things."

Arlene gave a quick nod. "A lot of Mama's things are still here, too, and we'll need to decide what to do with those."

"I'm so glad Doris found those birdhouses." Elsie paused. "I can't believe no one saw them in all the rubble before."

"I suppose they would have eventually been discovered, but it was perfect timing all the way around." Arlene stared at Dad's Sunday shoes, sitting by his dresser. "I believe Doris was right. Finding the birdhouses was meant to be."

"I may keep mine inside for a while," Elsie said. "I'd like to put it in a special place as a reminder of Mama and Dad."

"I may do the same thing," Arlene agreed.

Elsie sat on the end of the bed, viewing the clothes peeking out of the closet. "Maybe it would be best not to dispose of anything but the clothes until the will has been found. That way, if Dad specified anything in particular should go to certain people, we can respect his wishes."

"If there is a will." Arlene sighed. "Maybe Dad didn't make one."

"Jah, he did." Aunt Verna stepped into the room. "He told me the last time I came here for a visit."

"Did he say where he put it?" Elsie questioned.

Aunt Verna tipped her head. "What was that?"

Elsie repeated her question. It was amazing how sometimes Aunt Verna heard whatever had been said, while at other times people had to repeat themselves. *Perhaps I spoke too quietly. I need to make sure I speak loud enough and look in her direction when I'm talking to her.*

Aunt Verna moved closer. "My bruder said he'd made out a will, he even showed it to me. But . . ." her voice trailed off. "I can't remember now where he put it. Didn't he tell one of you about the will?"

Elsie and Arlene both shook their heads. "I'm sure he didn't tell Doris, either," Elsie said.

"And I'm even more certain he didn't tell our brother, because if he had, Joel would not have asked about the will," Arlene interjected.

"Maybe we need to box things up and wait until the will is found before deciding what to do with them." Elsie rose from the bed. "In the meantime, I'm *hungerich*. Should we stop and heat the casserole for lunch?"

"No need for that. The reason I came in here was to tell you I put the dish in the oven forty-five minutes ago. It's nice and warm and on the table." Aunt Verna smiled. "Lester's waiting for us, so why don't we join him?"

"Sounds good." Elsie and Arlene followed Aunt Verna out of Dad's room.

"Oh, before I forget, I wanted to ask you something." Aunt Verna paused in the hall, peering at them over the top of her glasses.

"What is it?" Elsie and Arlene asked in unison, stopping beside their aunt.

"I hate to ask, but if you happen to come across Eustace's worn-out boots, would you mind if I have them?" She pursed her lips. "It would be the ones held together by duct tape."

"Certainly." Elsie put her arm around her

aunt's shoulder.

"Danki." Aunt Verna wiped her eyes with the corner of her apron. "When I arrived last month to visit Eustace, I had to chuckle when I saw his old boots. I suggested he use duct tape to hold them together."

"They're probably in the barn somewhere. Even though he bought a new pair, I can't imagine he'd get rid of the old ones." Arlene paused, blinking against tears about to spill over. "He was wearing those new boots the day Larry and I found him."

"Well, your daed mentioned how he'd bought a pair of old cowboy boots at an auction one time and your mamm couldn't imagine why."

"I remember those," Elsie exclaimed. "Dad planted flowers in them."

"Jah, and he told me your mamm ended up liking the idea." Aunt Verna grinned. "So if you find those old duct-taped boots, I'd like to plant flowers in them. They hold a good memory for me of my bruder."

"We'd be pleased if you turned Dad's old boots into your own special memory." Arlene hugged Aunt Verna, and Elsie did the same.

When they entered the kitchen, Elsie stopped in mid-stride as soon as she saw Uncle Lester sitting in Dad's roll-about chair

WANDA *&.* BRUNSTETTER & JEAN BRUNSTETTER

at the head of the table. Her chin trembled as she pressed her hand to her chest. The tears didn't seem to want to stop today. The sight of Uncle Lester sitting in Dad's spot was a vivid reminder that he was gone and would never occupy his special chair again. She would miss seeing Dad roll around as he often did, going from room to room. It had become his trademark of sorts. Elsie blinked rapidly. *Oh, Dad, if only you hadn't gone up in the tree house.*

After lunch, Elsie helped put stuff away. "I'm going to walk to the phone shack and check for messages. I doubt Doris has called, but there may be a chance. I shouldn't be long." She headed out the door.

"Hey, wait up!" Arlene called. "I'll walk with you."

Elsie waited for her sister to catch up. "Oh, good, you can hunt for *schpinne* for me." She laughed.

Arlene snickered. "Well, it wouldn't be anything new. You could never handle it when a spider was in the bedroom we shared growing up. You'd say, 'Arlene, would you please take care of it for me? Schpinne are creepy.'"

"I can't deny it. I called on you a lot to do the nasty deed—only because Doris was too small, and the spiders were nearly as big as her." Elsie elbowed her sister, chuckling. It felt good to find something to smile about.

When they got to the phone shack, Arlene stepped in and brushed away a web. "No messages," she announced.

"Our sister must be doing okay. Guess we'd better get back to the house and box up some more stuff. I brought peanut butter cookies for us to snack on. I'll set them on the table soon." Elsie pushed a wayward strand of hair back under her head covering before linking arms with Arlene.

As they headed to the house, Elsie hummed a silly tune their father used to play on his harmonica. There were so many memories of Dad she would always treasure. Someday, she would see him again in heaven.

⁓

Akron

When Kristi got off work that afternoon, she didn't bother going home to change out of her nursing uniform; she headed straight for Joel's place, hoping he'd be there. She had to find out why he'd taken money from their account and thought it would be better if they talked face-to-face. She didn't know how she'd gotten through the day without

WANDA *&.* BRUNSTETTER & JEAN BRUNSTETTER

leaving early to confront Joel.

A light rain trickled down the windshield, so Kristi turned on her wipers. Listening to the steady *swish-swish* of the wiper blades, she thought about her perplexing relationship with Joel. *Could Mom be right about Joel? Maybe he's not a Christian. He could only be pretending to be one by going to church with me on Sundays. But it doesn't make sense. Joel grew up in the Amish church. He should be spiritually grounded.*

Kristi reflected on the information she'd found on the Internet. One site talked specifically about baptism and confession of faith. She'd learned those wishing to be baptized and join the Amish church must first take a series of instructional classes. On the Saturday before baptism took place, the candidates would be given the opportunity to change their mind.

I wonder why Joel didn't do that. Why'd he wait to leave until after he joined the church? There were so many unanswered questions.

Kristi had also learned from the website that during the baptismal service, each of the young men and women were asked three questions: (1) if they were willing to renounce the world and be obedient only to God and the church, (2) if they were willing to walk with Christ and His church and remain

92

faithful throughout their life, and (3) if they could confess Jesus Christ as the Son of God. They had to answer affirmatively to each question. Then the deacon poured water into the bishop's cupped hands, which he dripped over the candidate's head. The ritual of baptism signified the individual had formally become a member of the church.

"If Joel complied with all three things, how could he not be a Christian?" Kristi murmured. She pressed her lips tightly together. *But if Joel is a Christian, why is he ignoring his family and being deceitful with me? But then, we're only human, and everyone makes mistakes. I have my own faults to deal with.*

❧

The first thing Joel did when he got home from work was to take a shower and change his clothes. Following that, he went to the kitchen to make a sandwich, since he didn't feel like cooking.

Joel was about to sit down when he heard a car pull into the yard. Going to the window and looking out, he was surprised to see Kristi get out of her car, wearing her nurse's uniform.

He hurried to the door, hoping everything was okay. Normally Kristi called before coming over.

The minute she stepped onto the porch, Joel sensed something was wrong. No cute dimpled smile or friendly greeting. Kristi's lips were pressed into a white slash as she held tightly onto her purse.

"Come in before the wind blows rain under the porch eaves." Joel opened the door wider, and Kristi stepped inside.

He leaned down and pressed his lips against her cold cheek. "I'm surprised to see you. I didn't think we were getting together this evening. Is everything all right?"

"I–I'm not sure." Kristi opened her purse and pulled out a slip of paper. "I went to the bank on my way to work this morning. When I made a deposit to our savings account, I was given this." Kristi's hand shook as she handed it to him.

Joel didn't have to look at the deposit slip to know what was on it. The teller had printed the new balance on the back.

"Did you take money from our account without telling me?" Kristi's sharp tone hit Joel like a dagger.

He shuffled his feet a few times, while clearing his throat. "I. . .I admit, I did make a withdrawal, but you told me awhile back if I needed money I could borrow some from our account."

She looked up at him defiantly. "You assured me you would never take any of the money without telling me about it."

Joel gave his shirt collar a tug before rubbing the back of his neck. "Guess I must have forgotten to mention it. Sorry. I'll make sure it never happens again."

"What I would like to know is what kind of problems are you faced with that you would need to take over half the money we'd saved?" She continued to stare at him through squinted eyes.

Joel squirmed uncomfortably. He wasn't about to tell her that because he'd bought an expensive car he couldn't pay his subcontractors. She'd think he was a louse—not to mention a risky choice as a husband.

Joel clasped his fingers around her hand. He felt relief when she didn't pull away. "As you may recall, I lost out on a big job a few months ago, and it set me back."

She gave a slow nod. "You've been busy with work since then. I figured you were making enough to get caught up."

Heat rushed to his cheeks, and he let go of her hand. "I'm not. Most of the jobs I've taken on have been small and didn't pay a lot. To save money, I've done many of them myself."

Kristi's face softened some. "I wish you would have talked to me about this, Joel. Remember how I told you the speaker at the marriage seminar stressed the importance of communication?"

"Yeah, I know. I didn't want to worry you, though."

"I'm more worried about you pushing me out of your life." Her voice trembled.

Joel felt a sudden coldness deep inside. "I'm not pushing you out of my life, Kristi. I didn't want you to worry about something that was out of your control."

"We could have talked about it and prayed together. I love you, Joel. I want honesty and trust between us."

Joel pulled Kristi into his arms, holding her close. "I love you, too, sweetheart. Am I forgiven?"

"Yes," she murmured against his chest. "But from now on, no more secrets please."

Joel stroked her silky hair, then bent to kiss her lips. He hated keeping information from Kristi, but some things were best left unsaid.

CHAPTER 9

Wednesday evening, Kristi had finished eating supper when she heard the doorbell ring. Thinking it might be Joel, she hurried to answer it.

"Oh, hi," Kristi said, when she opened the door and saw her mother on the porch, holding a paper sack. "What are you doing out and about?" Kristi held the door open while her mother entered.

Mom stepped into the hall then turned to face Kristi. "Your dad had a deacon's meeting at the church this evening, so I seized the opportunity to come by and see your new wall hanging."

"It's draped over the back of the sofa in the living room." Kristi gave her mother a wide grin. "Come on in. I'm anxious to see what you think of it."

Mom handed Kristi the bag she held. "First, I have something for you."

"What's in here?" Kristi asked, peeking inside.

"I stopped at the market on my way over and got a few things I thought you might like—apples, a butternut squash, and some spareribs they had on special."

"Thanks Mom. I'll take these things to the kitchen and put the meat in the fridge. If you'd like to come along, I'll pour us a glass of cider."

Mom smacked her lips. "Sounds good. I love cider this time of the year."

"Same here."

When they finished up in the kitchen and started for the living room, Mom paused and tipped her head. "Kristi, you look like you've lost some weight."

"You think so?" Kristi wasn't about to admit she had lost a few pounds from all the stress of worrying over Joel and their relationship. Needing to change the topic, she hurried into the other room and pointed toward the couch. "There's the quilted wall hanging Joel's sister gave me. What do you think?"

"It's lovely." Mom slid her fingers across the material. "How could she part with such a beautiful family heirloom?"

"Each of Joel's sisters has her own. Doris said their mother made even more, so it's not like I was given the only one."

Mom removed her jacket and took a seat on the sofa. "How come you haven't hung the quilt on the wall?"

"I'm waiting until after Joel and I are married. Then we can decide where we want to hang it in our house." Kristi sat beside her mother.

"How are things between you and Joel these days?" Mom inquired.

"We're going on a picnic after church this Sunday." Kristi's stomach tightened. No way was she going to tell her mother about Joel taking money from their joint account. It would give her one more reason to question his ability to be a good husband. She would probably say Joel was deceitful and couldn't be trusted. Lately, Kristi had to admit, she felt the same way, but her love for him always won out. He'd apologized for taking the money, and Kristi was confident he wouldn't do it again.

"I hoped you hadn't made any plans for Sunday afternoon." Mom touched Kristi's arm. "I planned to ask if you and Joel could come over to our house to eat after church. Your dad mentioned it's been some time since we've visited with both of you."

"Can we do it next Sunday instead? Joel called last night and said he has something special to give me, and he'd probably prefer being alone." Kristi had a suspicion Joel might be planning to give her an engagement ring, but wondered how he could afford it, given his financial circumstances. *If it is a ring, I hope*

he didn't charge it, or we'll be stuck with making
payments for a long time.

As eager as Kristi was to make their engagement official and set a wedding date, she didn't want to start their marriage deeply in debt. She'd been praying Joel would land a big job soon and be able to replace what he'd taken from their account. Surely, with all the building going on in the area, something would open up.

"Next Sunday will be fine." Mom rested her arm on the sofa pillow. "We can confirm it when the time gets closer and you've had a chance to speak with Joel. He might not be interested in having lunch with us."

Kristi couldn't imagine why he wouldn't. After all, Mom and Dad would be his in-laws once she and Joel were married.

❧

Berlin, Ohio

"Are you feeling all right, Doris?" Brian motioned to her half-eaten supper plate. "You've barely touched your food."

Doris exhaled as she pushed her beef stew around with a fork. "My stomach is queasy and has been all day. This flu bug I came down with on Monday is determined to stick around. I may have picked something up the day of the funeral with so many people around."

"Maybe it's not the flu. Have you called the doctor and told him your symptoms?"

"No, but if I had called, he'd probably tell me all the usual things to do for the flu—drink lots of fluids and get plenty of rest—which is what I've been doing."

Brian touched her forehead. "You don't have a fever. Do you feel achy?"

"No, only my stomach's upset."

His eyes darkened, and a sly grin appeared on his lips. "You don't suppose. . . ."

"Suppose what?" Doris reached for her glass of water and took a sip.

"Is it possible? . . . After all this time, could you be having morning sickness because you're expecting a boppli?"

"I don't think so, Brian. Besides, the nausea I've felt isn't just in the mornings. Sometimes it lasts all day."

"Have you talked to your sisters to get their opinion? They've both experienced what it's like to be pregnant. I'm sure they'd know if what some folks call 'morning sickness' could occur at other times of the day."

"I suppose I could ask them." Doris fiddled with the napkin beside her plate. "But I'm sure it's a lingering flu bug." She forced herself to take another bite of stew and closed her eyes. *Wouldn't it be something if I was actually pregnant? I won't get my hopes up, but it would truly be a miracle and an answer to prayer.*

❧

Akron

Joel leaned back in the recliner and checked his phone messages. There were two from people asking for bids on small jobs, and a message from Elsie saying the will had not been found.

He leaped from the chair and started to pace. *This is ridiculous! How long can it take for my sisters to find Dad's will? There are three of them, after all, plus Aunt Verna and Uncle Lester, if they decided to stick around awhile.*

Joel had half a mind to get in the car and go over to his dad's house and search for the will himself. But he didn't feel like making the hour's drive, since Charm was more than sixty miles away. It would take too much time to drive there, search the house for the will, and drive back home. If at all possible, he wanted to hit the hay early tonight. Right now, he had a few jobs lined up, which he needed to get started on early tomorrow and Friday. Fortunately, he'd given a few of his subcontractors part of the money he still owed them, so they'd agreed to do the jobs Joel couldn't do, such as the wiring and plumbing.

He stopped pacing long enough to grab his cup of coffee and take a drink. *If I don't hear anything from Elsie by the time those two jobs are finished, I may drive over to Millersburg and talk to her in person.*

This Sunday, Joel would be taking Kristi on a picnic, and he'd like to tell her the will had been found. With the exception of his relationship with Kristi, it was hard to find much good in his life these days. " 'Course, there's also my beautiful Corvette," he mumbled. "Think I'll get it out right now and take a short spin." Looking at his watch, Joel realized he still had enough time to go out and be back in plenty of time for bed. One thing Joel had discovered since he'd gotten the classic car: driving around in it helped him to relax and forget his troubles—if only for a little while.

❧

Millersburg

Elsie had been thinking about Doris and was considering going to Berlin to see how she was, but the day had gotten away from her. She'd rushed about cleaning; had stripped all their beds; and washed sheets, towels, and clothes. Now it was time to get supper on the table.

Her thoughts jumped to Joel, another family member to be concerned about. *Dad was right. Joel acts spoiled and only thinks of himself.*

Elsie paused in the hall and took a couple of deep breaths to calm herself before going to the kitchen. She still had some laundry to take down from the clothesline, so she asked Mary to get it.

"Sure, Mom, I'll do it right now."

On entering the kitchen, Elsie was pleased to see Hope peeling potatoes and putting them into a kettle for boiling. The roast was in the oven, and Elsie had sliced some tomatoes she'd picked from the garden this morning. So far, they'd had no frost, and if the weather held out, they could get tomatoes for a few more weeks. John was home from work and was out in the barn with the boys, so they would eat soon after they came in from doing their chores.

Hope dropped a potato into the kettle and turned to face Elsie. "I miss Grandpa so much." Tears welled in her eyes.

"I do, too." Elsie gave her youngest daughter's shoulder a tender squeeze. "Let's try to remember all the good times we had with him."

"I will, but it's hard knowing both he and Grandma Byler are gone."

Elsie's eyes filled with tears as she gave her daughter a hug.

"Hey, are you two all right?" John asked when he stepped in from outside.

Elsie patted her damp eyes. "We miss my daed."

"We all do." John moved closer and rubbed Elsie's back.

She sniffed. "Did you get all the chores done? Where are the boys?"

"They're feeding the cats. I told 'em to hurry. Oh, and I checked phone messages. There was one from Doris."

"What did she say?"

"Said she's felt nauseated off and on all day." His forehead wrinkled. "She's been *grank* for a few days now. Has she seen the doctor?"

"I'm not sure. I'll give her a call after supper."

"Might be a good idea." John sniffed the air. "Dinner smells good. How long till we eat?"

"Fifteen minutes, maybe," Hope spoke up. "As soon as the potatoes have cooked."

"I'll go out and hurry the boys. Then we'll all wash up."

Elsie watched out the window as her husband returned to the barn. *I wonder what's going on with Doris.* She thought back to when she was expecting. *Could my little sister be pregnant?*

"I got the clean laundry off the line and brought in." Mary bounded into the kitchen.

"Danki." Elsie placed a serving fork on the table for the meat. "After you wash your hands, would you please help your sister set the table?"

"Sure, Mom." Mary headed down the hall toward the bathroom.

Elsie was sure her oldest daughter missed her grandfather, too, but she seemed to be holding it inside, going about her business as though everything was normal.

Elsie leaned against the counter and closed her eyes. *We all need to grieve—even Joel. I hope he feels some remorse for the way he talked to Dad when he was alive.*

CHAPTER 10

Akron

"What a beautiful day for a picnic." Kristi sighed as she set her wicker basket on the blanket Joel had spread on the grass. "Fall is my favorite time of the year. Look how pretty the leaves are getting." Kristi pointed to a grove of sugar maples with leaves of red, orange, and yellow.

Joel stared blankly at them as he took a seat on the blanket beside her. He didn't seem interested in the beautiful trees. He had been quiet and pensive ever since church let out. Kristi wished she could read his mind.

"Before we start eating, I have something for you." Joel reached into the pocket of his denim jeans and pulled out a small velveteen box.

Kristi's heart quickened as he placed it in her hand.

"Go ahead. Open it." Joel's sudden smile caused her heart to beat a little faster.

Kristi's fingers trembled as she untied the ribbon. When she opened the lid, an attractive pair of pink earrings, sparkling in the sun, peeked out at her. She lowered her head, staring intently at them. Although disappointed he hadn't given her a ring, in one sense Kristi felt relief. She was certain Joel hadn't spent nearly as much on the earrings as he would on a diamond ring, which meant he hadn't put himself in financial jeopardy.

"They're beautiful, Joel. Thank you," Kristi murmured. "But you didn't have to get me a gift. It's not my birthday or anything."

He smiled. "It's a token of my affection, and a reminder of how much I love you."

"I love you, too." She closed the box and put it inside the picnic basket.

"Aren't you going to wear them?"

"Not right now. I'll save them for a special occasion." She reached for his hand.

He leaned over and gave her a kiss. "Should we eat? I'm hungry."

"Of course. Should we pray the Amish way before I take out the food?"

"Sure, that's fine." Joel bowed his head, and Kristi did the same.

When they finished silent praying, Kristi handed Joel a paper plate and got out the bucket of chicken they'd picked up on the way. They also had bottles of sparkling lemon water, as well as some sliced veggies she had fixed this morning.

As they ate, Kristi noticed how quiet it

was. Except for her and Joel, no one was at this end of the park. Sitting there, with no noise except the chatter of a few birds, she almost felt Amish. No cars were in sight, since the parking lot was farther down the path. Everything in their presence was natural and seemed like a gift from God.

Don't be silly. Kristi chided herself for feeling Amish. *You're living in a fantasy world.* She had to admit there was something about the Amish she found enchanting. She didn't want to idealize them, though. Like people from all walks of life, the Amish had their share of troubles, and none of them were perfect. Still, Kristi admired their values, love for their family, and dedication to a way of life that had been established hundreds of years ago. They worked hard, but their lives were simplified, without all the gadgets the English world seemed to need.

"A nickel for your thoughts." Joel tweaked Kristi's nose.

"I was thinking about your Amish heritage and wishing I could incorporate more of their ways into my life."

Joel's brows lowered. "Now don't tell me you've decided to start hanging your laundry out to dry or get rid of your computer and TV."

She swatted his arm playfully. "I may not

give them up, but there are other things I'd rather do than watch TV or hang out on the Internet reading posts on social media sites. Truthfully speaking, I believe I could live without either of them."

"What would you like to do?"

Kristi held up her index finger. "For one thing, I'd like to learn some Pennsylvania Dutch words." She leaned in closer to him and lowered her voice. "Would you teach me, Joel?"

His nose wrinkled. "What for? The Amish world is no longer part of my life. It's behind me."

"No, it's not. You still have family who remained Amish. When they're speaking Pennsylvania Dutch, I'd like to understand what they're saying."

Joel grunted. "You don't realize what you're asking. It would take years for you to learn the language well enough to grasp it."

Unwilling to give in, Kristi folded her arms. "Could you at least teach me to say a few words?"

"I suppose, but I don't see much point in it."

"You might be surprised what a quick learner I am." She smiled. "Give me a couple of words and tell me their meaning."

"What? Now?"

"Uh-huh. There's no time like the present."

"Okay, here's an easy one. Jah. It means yes."

"That's easy to remember. What else?"

"*Gut* is for good, and danki for thanks."

"Jah, gut, danki," Kristi repeated the words. "Now give me a sentence to learn."

Joel rolled his eyes. "Okay, but then let's talk about something else."

"That's fine."

Speaking slowly, Joel pronounced each word clearly. *"Geld zwingt die welt."*

"What does it mean?"

"Money rules the world." He bobbed his head. "And I have to say it's true."

"It doesn't have to be," Kristi argued. "There are many things we should focus on rather than money—important things like our relationships with people."

Joel folded his arms. *"Humph!* Some people I can't have a relationship with."

"Are you thinking of anyone in particular?"

"My brother-in-law, for one." Joel frowned. "John should have stayed out of Elsie's and my discussion the day of Dad's funeral. The subject of Dad's will was between her and me."

"If you were married and someone talked to your wife the way you did Elsie, wouldn't you step in and say something?"

Joel shrugged his shoulders. "It all depends on what was being said. If it was something that didn't pertain to me, I'd keep quiet." Joel grabbed his bottle of sparkling water and took a drink. "Okay, that's enough for now. Let's talk about something else."

"Have you spoken to any of your family since the funeral?" Kristi asked.

He shook his head. "Got a message from Elsie, though. Said she'd let me know when they found Dad's will. It's been over a week since his funeral, and I haven't heard a thing."

"They may not have found it yet, and they're most likely busy with other things." Kristi repositioned herself on the blanket. "I wish you weren't putting so much emphasis on getting some of your father's money. Have you even grieved your loss? Don't you feel sad that he's gone?"

Joel set his bottle down and looked right at Kristi. "I'm sorry he died, but there was no love lost between me and my dad. He didn't give a hoot about me."

Kristi's heart went out to Joel. She could see by his pained expression that he was miserable. Harboring ill feelings toward anyone, let alone a parent, could do nothing but tear a person down. If Joel didn't rise above his anger and forgive his father, he would never be at peace.

She touched his arm. "Have you prayed about this? Have you asked God to help you with your feelings of bitterness?"

Joel's face flamed like a bonfire being lit. "I don't need any lectures, Kristi. And I sure don't need you preaching at me."

"I wasn't. I'm only trying to offer my support."

"Support is fine. I don't appreciate being preached at, though." He rubbed his hand against his cheek. "I got enough lectures from my dad to last a lifetime." Grabbing the empty tub the chicken had been in, Joel tossed it into the wicker basket. "You know what, Kristi? We need to go. I have some things to do at home before I go to work tomorrow."

All Kristi could do was nod. How could such a pleasant day have turned sour so quickly? Maybe she ought to give Joel some time to mull over the things they'd discussed. Surely after he'd had a chance to analyze his behavior he would realize he was wrong.

Later in the day after Joel dropped Kristi off at her condo, he'd gone home and taken the Corvette out of his shop. Since he'd washed the car the day before, Joel wanted to get a fresh coat of wax on so it would shine even more.

As Joel began working on the hood, he thought about the things Kristi said to him at the park. She'd meant well when she suggested he pray about his bitterness, but Joel didn't put much stock in prayer. *I shouldn't have gotten so upset with her. She probably thinks I'm mad. I'll give her a call as soon as I'm done with the car and try to smooth things over.*

Joel moved to the back of the car and was almost finished waxing when he heard a car coming up his driveway. As soon as he realized it was Kristi, he panicked. *I can't let her see the Vette. If she sees the car, I'll have some explaining to do.*

Joel reached in his pocket and fumbled with his keys. But he couldn't get them out quickly enough, let alone get in the car and start it up. Kristi had already seen him.

"What are you doing with Tom's car?" she asked after she'd parked her car and gotten out. "Is he here? Did you two have something planned for today? Is that why you wanted to leave the park in such a hurry?" Kristi glanced around.

Tom's car? Why would she think it's his Corvette? Then Joel remembered Kristi had seen him and Tom together with the car one night several weeks ago. He couldn't say Tom was here. She might want to talk to him. Then what? Joel needed to come up with some excuse as to why he was waxing the car Kristi thought belonged to Tom, without him being present. Or he could come right out and tell her the truth. Kristi had made it clear she didn't appreciate being lied to, so maybe it would be best to admit the Corvette was his. First, though, he needed to find out why she was here.

"I'm surprised to see you. Why'd you come by?" he asked, avoiding her question.

"I left my cell phone in your car."

"Oh, I'll get it for you right now." Joel left the chamois on the Corvette's hood and raced into the garage. When he returned with Kristi's cell phone, he found her staring at the Vette. "This looks like an expensive car. Tom must be making good money."

Joel's face heated. "Actually, the car's not Tom's."

"Oh? Who owns it then?"

"I do."

Kristi's posture stiffened. "This is your car?"

"Yeah."

"But I thought. . ." Her eyes blinked rapidly. "How come you let me believe it was Tom's?"

Sweat beaded on Joel's forehead and dripped onto his cheeks. "The thing is. . .I got the car at an auction back in August, and I paid a hefty price for it."

"Is that why you took money from our account—to pay for this?" Kristi's voice quivered as she pointed at the car.

Joel shook his head forcefully. "I used money I'd gotten from a big job for the car—money I'd planned to use to pay my subcontractors."

Her mouth twisted. "How could you do something like that, Joel?"

"Figured I could make up the money when I got paid for another job I'd bid on." Joel grimaced. "Unfortunately, I didn't get the second job, which left me in a bind. So in order to pay some of the men who'd worked for me, I borrowed money from our savings account."

Kristi's hand shook as she motioned to the Corvette. "So all this time, you've had the car and never said a word to me about it?"

Joel's face tightened as he lowered his head. "Sorry, Kristi. Guess I haven't been thinking straight lately."

"You're right, you haven't! I can't believe you would be so deceitful." She choked on her words. "Don't you care about anyone but yourself?"

Joel moved toward Kristi and grasped her wrist. "I care about you."

"Let go of me!" She pulled her arm toward herself, but Joel gripped it tighter.

"No, Kristi, I need you to listen to me."

"Do you really care, Joel? If you did, you wouldn't sneak around behind my back and do whatever you pleased." Kristi's chin quivered as tears pooled in her eyes. "I looked past you taking money from our account and not telling me about your Amish heritage until your father died, but another deception is too much."

"What are you saying?"

Kristi turned her head away from him, remaining silent for a few minutes. She sniffled before speaking again. "It. . .it's time for us to go our separate ways."

"You can't mean it, Kristi." Desperation welled in Joel's chest. "You're angry right now. Please give me another chance and let me explain a little more."

"You've already explained. There's nothing more to be said. You've kept too many things hidden from me." Using her free hand, she pried Joel's fingers loose. "Without honesty, our relationship will never work. I'm sorry, Joel, but we're done."

A sense of panic welled in his soul as he watched Kristi get into her car. "Kristi, please wait!"

After she slammed her door shut, Joel

could do nothing but watch Kristi back out of his driveway. He fell to his knees, his body hunched over, as he tried to choke down a sob. *Why? Why?* His nails bit into his palms. Heat flushed through his body, and he pounded his fists against the gravel. *Haven't I had enough to deal with?* He glared up at the sky. "Well, haven't I?"

Once Joel calmed down a bit, he headed up to his trailer house. His hand trembled as he reached for the doorknob. *It can't end like this. I need to get her back. There has to be a way.*

Wanda E. Brunstetter

New York Times bestselling award-winning author Wanda E. Brunstetter is one of the founders of the Amish fiction genre. Wanda's ancestors were part of the Anabaptist faith, and her novels are based on personal research intended to accurately portray the Amish way of life. Her books are well-read and trusted by many Amish, who credit her for giving readers a deeper understanding of the Amish people and their customs. When Wanda visits her Amish friends, she finds herself drawn to their peaceful lifestyle, sincerity, and close family ties. Wanda enjoys photography, ventriloquism, gardening, bird-watching, beachcombing, and spending time with her family. She and her husband, Richard, have been blessed with two grown children, six grandchildren, and two great-grandchildren.

To learn more about Wanda, visit her website at www.wandabrunstetter.com.

Jean Brunstetter

Jean Brunstetter became fascinated with the Amish when she first went to Pennsylvania to visit her father-in-law's family. Since that time, Jean has become friends with several Amish families and enjoys writing about their way of life. She also likes to put some of the simple practices followed by the Amish into her daily routine. Jean lives in Washington State with her husband, Richard Jr., and their three children, but takes every opportunity to visit Amish communities in several states. In addition to writing, Jean enjoys boating, gardening, and spending time on the beach.

The story of The Amish Millionaire
continues with…

The Missing Will
Part 4

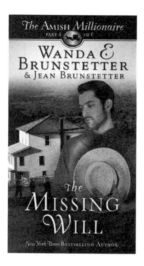

In *The Missing Will*, the Byler family is on a hunt for their father's will while relations continue to deteriorate among the siblings and between Joel and his fiancée. Joel is desperate for closure to his father's estate, but how far is he willing to go in order to restore the chaotic turn his life has taken? Will his quest cause him to ignore the needs of those closest to him?

DON'T MISS A SINGLE BOOK IN THIS
EXCLUSIVE 6-BOOK SERIAL NOVEL

AVAILABLE AT YOUR FAVORITE BOOKSTORE

OTHER BOOKS BY
WANDA E. BRUNSTETTER

Adult Fiction

The Prairie State Friends Series
The Decision
The Gift
The Restoration
The Half-Stitched Amish Quilting Club
The Tattered Quilt
The Healing Quilt

The Discovery Saga
Goodbye to Yesterday
The Silence of Winter
The Hope of Spring
The Pieces of Summer
A Revelation in Autumn
A Vow for Always

Kentucky Brothers Series
The Journey
The Healing
The Struggle

Brides of Lehigh Canal Series
Kelly's Chance
Betsy's Return
Sarah's Choice

Woman of Courage
The Lopsided Christmas Cake—with Jean Brunstetter

Children's Fiction

Double Trouble
What a Pair!
Bumpy Ride Ahead
Bubble Troubles
Green Fever
Humble Pie

Rachel Yoder—Always Trouble Somewhere
8-Book Series

The Wisdom of Solomon

Nonfiction

Wanda E. Brunstetter's Amish Friends Cookbook
Wanda E. Brunstetter's Amish Friends Cookbook Vol. 2
The Best of Amish Friends Cookbook Collection
Wanda E. Brunstetter's Desserts Cookbook
Wanda E. Brunstetter's Amish Christmas Cookbook
The Simple Life Devotional
A Celebration of the Simple Life Devotional
Portrait of Amish Life—with Richard Brunstetter
Simple Life Perpetual Calendar—with Richard Brunstetter

JUL - - 2020